THE CHEROKEE
TRAIL

THE CHEROKEE TRAIL

LOUIS L'AMOUR

BANTAM BOOKS
NEW YORK • TORONTO • LONDON • SYDNEY • AUCKLAND

THE CHEROKEE TRAIL
A Bantam Book
Published simultaneously in hardcover and rack-size
paperback by Bantam / August 1982
An Alternate Selection of Doubleday Book Club / August 1982
The Louis L'Amour Hardcover Collection / August 1982

If you want to purchase more of these titles, please write to:
The Louis L'Amour Collection
1745 Broadway
New York, NY 10019

ISBN 0-553-06242-5

Published simultaneously in the United States and Canada

---

*Bantam Books are published by Bantam Books, a division of Bantam
Doubleday Dell Publishing Group, Inc. Its trademark, consisting of
the words "Bantam Books" and the portrayal of a rooster, is
Registered in U.S. Patent and Trademark Office and in other
countries. Marca Registrada. Bantam Books, 1745 Broadway, New
York, New York 10019.*

PRINTED IN THE UNITED STATES OF AMERICA
0   9   8   7   6   5

To Harry and Ruth

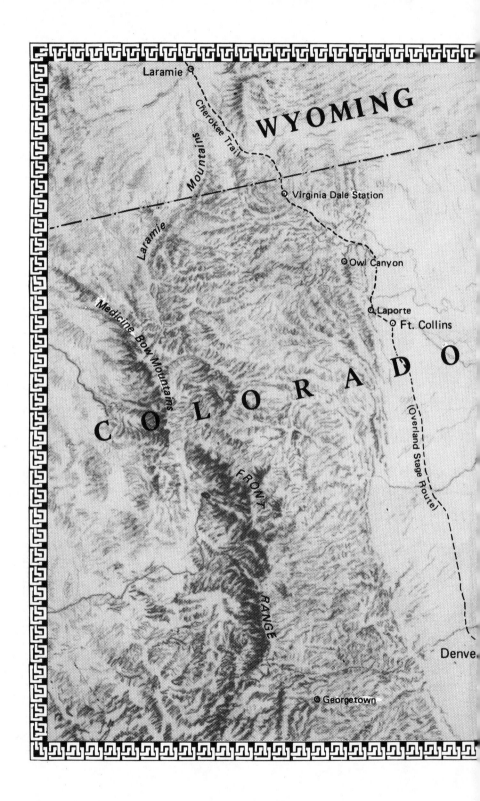

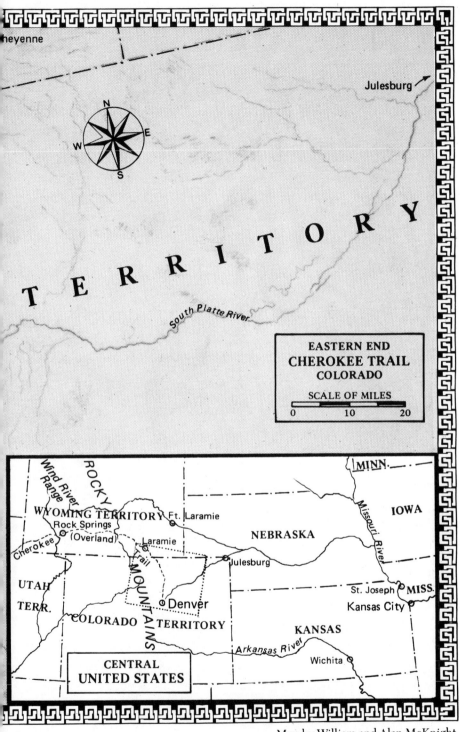

heyenne

Julesburg

N
W · E
S

TERRITORY

South Platte River

EASTERN END
CHEROKEE TRAIL
COLORADO

SCALE OF MILES

0   10   20

Wind River Range
ROCKY
WYOMING TERRITORY   Ft. Laramie
Rock Springs
(Overland)   Laramie
Cherokee
MOUNTAINS
Julesburg
Trail
UTAH
TERR.
Denver
COLORADO   TERRITORY
CENTRAL
UNITED STATES

MINN.
IOWA
Missouri River
NEBRASKA
St. Joseph   MISS.
Kansas City
KANSAS
Arkansas River
Wichita

Map by William and Alan McKnight

Author's Note

The Cherokee Trail received its name from a party of Cherokee Indians who went over the route in 1848–1849, bound for the gold fields in California. According to the best reports, their interest lay less in the discovery of gold than in locating a home for their people. Finding the turmoil of the gold rush not to their liking, the Cherokees returned by approximately the same route.

When the Civil War pulled away most of the soldiers guarding the Overland Stage, that part of the route from Laramie to Julesburg was abandoned due to continual Indian attacks, and the stage was routed south to Denver and then over the Cherokee Trail to Laramie.

My story is concerned with that portion of the trail that runs north from Denver through Laporte to Laramie. North of Laporte, this is wide-open country for much of the way, and the old stage station at Virginia Dale is still standing.

Outlaws did have a hideout, used occasionally, in a natural rock fortress in the hills west of Owl Canyon.

The Cherokees found gold in several of the creeks along the way, which was one of the factors that led to the gold rush to Colorado.

ONE

When the stage slowed to allow the horses to walk up the long grade, Mary Breydon was the only passenger awake. Or so she believed. There was no telling about the man with the hat over his face. Several times during the night, she had seen him move, and his movements did not seem to be those of a sleeping man.

Feeble yellow-gray light was filtering through the fly-specked, dust-filmed windows. She peered out.

The rolling brown hills were beginning to take shape from the darkness. It seemed a harsh and barren land, this new home of hers, its monotony broken only by occasional outcroppings of craggy sandstone. Somewhere farther west lay the front range of the Rockies, of which she caught an occasional glimpse beyond the low hills.

Aside from Mary and her daughter, Peg, there were four passengers caught in the awkward, uncomfortable positions of people trying to sleep on seats designed only for sitting.

The man with a black hat over his eyes sat in the back of the coach beside Peg and herself. Before he had gone to sleep,

1

she had seen him as a lean, hawk-featured young man with a level, direct gaze from eyes that never seemed to smile. He wore a dark, shabby coat, a plaid shirt, gray pants, and a pistol in a tied-down holster. When he shifted position, she glimpsed a second gun tucked behind his belt, butt forward. A new Henry rifle leaned against the wall of the coach at his side.

She recognized the rifle at once, although she had little knowledge of such things. She remembered how pleased her husband had been when he had been able to purchase one, and that rifle was now wrapped in a roll of her bedding atop the stage.

Opposite him sat a well-dressed young man in a checkered vest. When he was awake, he had kept trying to catch her eye, and he had a bold, insinuating expression she found difficult to avoid, for whenever she lifted her eyes he was looking right at her.

The other man on the stage was stocky and powerfully built, wearing a short beard and a store-bought suit. He also carried a gun on his left side, butt forward. The only other person on the stage was an Irish girl only two or three years younger than herself.

As if sensing Mary's gaze, the Irish girl opened her eyes. She glanced at Peg, who was sleeping with her head on Mary's shoulder.

"It's a fine lass you have there, mum."

"A very tired one, I'm afraid."

"You've come a long way, then?"

"From Virginia."

"Ah? 'Tis where the fighting is? This War Between the States they talk of?"

"Yes, it is. We've seen some of it."

Peg stirred, sat up, and rubbed her eyes. "Mother? Is it much further?"

"Only a little further. We're almost there."

The heavy-set man glanced at her. "Don't expect much at Cherokee, ma'am. The station's the worst run on the route. It ain't like Ben Holladay to let it get so run-down."

He peered from the window, then added, "The food's scarcely fit to eat, and Scant Luther, who operates the station, is a mean, brutal man who's drunk half the time. A fine-looking woman like you shouldn't even get off the stage."

The man in the checkered vest leaned toward her. "Don't I know you from some place? You sure look—"

"No." Her tone was definite. "You do not know me. We have never met."

"But I—"

From under the brim of the black hat, the voice was abrupt, impatient. "You heard the lady, mister. She said you hadn't met. You haven't."

The man in the checkered vest flushed angrily. "I don't think—!"

"That's right, mister, you don't think. If I was you, I'd start thinkin', right now. Think slow and careful. In this country, when a lady says she doesn't know you, she doesn't. Also, it is likely she doesn't want to know you."

The man's lips parted as if to make an angry retort, but the one gray eye he could see was like looking down the barrel of a gun. His face tightened with anger, but some vague intuition of danger caused him to keep silent.

The heavy-set man's eyes met Mary's, showing faint, shared amusement. "Scant Luther runs the roughest station on the route, ma'am, and he keeps a bad crowd around him. Always drinking and fighting.

"Mark Stacy—he's the division agent—he told me Ben Holladay wanted Luther fired, but he was waiting for his replacement."

"Did he say who the replacement was to be?"

"Yes, ma'am, he did. He's hired a former soldier, Major M. O. Breydon, formerly of the U.S. Cavalry. Seems the major was invalided out of the army. He'd applied for the job."

Her eyes met his. "I am Mrs. Breydon. I am also M. O. Breydon. The major was killed by guerrillas a few weeks ago, and I am taking the job in his place."

There was a moment of astonished silence, and then the Irish girl spoke. "Ma'am, beggin' your pardon, I am, but you don't know what you're saying! You an' that sweet little girl in such a place! It's not to be thought of! You can't be serious, ma'am!"

"Indeed I am. I am very serious. Nor do I have a choice. A part of the Battle of Bull Run was fought across our plantation. Our buildings were burned and our stock run off. When the war is over, we shall go back, but now I have to make a living."

"Scant Luther," the heavy-set man warned, "is a very disagreeable man. Most of us respect womenfolks, but Luther is drunk half the time."

"He will have no reason to stay after I dismiss him. I am sure we will have no trouble."

"You'll soon know, ma'am," the heavy-set man commented. "That's it, right ahead!"

Mary Breydon leaned forward to see better. They were racing along a road through a small but lovely green valley scattered with trees. Before them was a cluster of gray, weather-beaten buildings, a corral, and more trees.

As they rolled to a stop at the station, the door banged open, and a big, slovenly man in his shirt-sleeves emerged. "Howdy, Wilbur! Get down an' have a drink! Tell the folks to come right on in!"

"We're runnin' behind time, Scant. Where's the team?"

"Aw, don't get yourself in a sweat! They'll be along! Come on in; grub's on the table!"

Wilbur Pattishal stepped down from the box. "Scant, we've no time to spare. I want that team out here, and I want them now."

Luther turned around slowly. "Well, now. If you're in such an almighty hurry, you just go get 'em yourself!"

Two or three rough-looking men were standing about, one of them with a bottle in his hand. He laughed.

Mary Breydon stepped from the coach, drawing all eyes. In her hands, she held an open letter that she handed to Wilbur.

"Mr. Pattishal? Will you read that, please? Read it aloud."

Wilbur glanced at the letter, then looked around and cleared his throat.

To Whom It May Concern:
This letter is authorization for M. O. Breydon to proceed to
Cherokee Station and upon arrival to take over its operation. It
also authorizes M. O. Breydon to discharge Scant Luther and
such others as Breydon shall deem necessary.

Mark Stacy
Division Agent

In the moment of startled silence that followed, Mary Breydon said, "Mr. Luther, you are discharged. You will vacate the premises immediately, removing only such articles as belong to you personally."

Luther stared, then laughed. "Ma'am, you're makin' a ruddy fool of yourself! No woman can run a station on the Cherokee Trail! Why this here's the roughest—

"There's Injuns, outlaws. Ma'am, you wouldn't last two days!"

"We are not discussing my qualifications, Mr. Luther. You are discharged. I suggest you take what is yours and leave. And please!" She gestured toward the hangers-on. "Take these with you!"

For a moment, she thought he would strike her. He took a half step forward, then glanced to the right and left. The heavy-set man stood, hands on his hips, watching. So did Wilbur Pattishal.

Then, for the first time, Luther seemed to see the man in the black hat standing to one side, alone. Something in his manner, in the very way he stood, warned Luther to be careful. He glanced at the man again, then his own stubbornness took control. He backed up and sat down in the doorway, blocking it.

"All right, lady, if you figure you can fire me, you just go right ahead and do it! This here's betwixt you an' me. If you're good enough to run this station, you're good enough to fire me. You just have at it."

He gestured to his men. "These here men are out of it, an'

so are those who come in on the stage. If they step in, there'll be some shootin', an' somebody will get killed.

"Now I say you ain't goin' in there. Not you or anybody else least I say so, and I—"

She moved so quickly it caught them unawares. One step and she had the whip from Wilbur's hand. It had a four-and-a-half-foot stock and an eight-foot braided lash, and the moment she took it in her hand, it was obvious she knew how to handle a whip.

She struck swiftly. The whip cracked like the report of a pistol, and the buckskin popper on the end of the lash bit flesh from Scant Luther's neck. With a cry of pain and startled anger, he lunged to his feet, and the second blow of the lash took him over the shoulders, the third on his leg.

He swore and lunged toward her, but she stepped quickly aside and struck again. Turning, he ran in a stumbling run, the popper ripping his shirt with one last blow.

Luther stumbled and fell. For a moment, he lay in the dust, and Mary gathered her whip. "Mr. Luther," she spoke quietly, "you are discharged."

Slowly, he got up from the ground. The man in the black hat had turned casually, facing him and, beyond him, his men. Blood trickled down his neck, and there was a livid streak across his shoulder and back.

"I'm goin', ma'am, but I'll be back. You can depend on it. When you least expect me, I'll be back."

Ignoring him, she turned toward the passengers. "If you people will wait, I'll see what there is to eat."

One of the men had lingered, and now she turned her attention to him. "Is there something you want?"

"I'm the stock tender, ma'am. What of it?"

"You've got five minutes to get that team out here and hooked up. Otherwise, you can start down the road."

He put his hands on his hips. "Now what if I did just that?"

"I'd hitch the team myself, and I'd pass your name to Ben Holladay. You'd never work another day from St. Joe to Sacramento."

He stared at her; then his eyes fell, and he walked away toward the stable.

She went inside the station and stopped, appalled.

The table was stacked high with dirty dishes, and on the very end of the table were some empty plates and a plate of steaks swimming in grease.

More dirty dishes were stacked in the sink. In a corner was a pair of worn boots caked with dried mud, and several dusty coats hung from nails driven into the wall. At a window, a dirty curtain hung from a broken rod.

Taking off her jacket, she rolled up her sleeves and went to work. First she opened the shutters on the other windows and let light stream into the room; then she put water on to boil and, taking a broom, began sweeping up the worst of the mess.

When the water was hot, she washed enough dishes to feed the few passengers and the stage driver.

The man in the black hat appeared in the door. "Don't worry about me, ma'am. I'll get something to eat later."

"You're not going on the stage?"

"No, ma'am. A man left a horse here for me. I figured to pick him up an' ride on." He paused. "Gettin' late to start a long ride. Maybe I'll just throw my bed on the grass under that tree, just for tonight," he added as he moved off.

"Mum?" The Irish girl stood in the doorway. "My name is Matty Maginnis. If you'd let me, I'd be glad to help. I've done a sight of it in my time."

"Please, would you?"

When they were working, washing dishes, cleaning up, Mary asked, "Are you going far, Matty?"

"Rock Springs Station if there's no work in Laramie."

"If it is a job you want, why not stay here and work for me? I'll need somebody to help around and to cook."

"I'll do it, mum, and pleased for the chance."

Working swiftly, they wiped off the benches and the table, put clean dishes in place, and dumped out the greasy steaks Luther had provided. It needed a little longer, but when they sat down, it was to a meal they could enjoy.

It was when she went to the door to call the passengers to the table that she saw the boy.

He was standing alone by the corner of the barn. He looked tired, and he looked hungry. He was shabbily dressed and barefooted. Suspended from a cord around his neck was a pair of boots, man's boots, hand stitched and polished.

TWO

"You got you a visitor," the man in the black hat commented. "Looks kind of all in."

"Young man?" she called.

He did not respond, just stood there looking at her. Who was he? A son of one of the hangers-on? Of Luther's perhaps?

She knew a little about boys. Not much, but a little. "What's the matter?" she asked. "Are you afraid of me?"

He came toward her. "I ain't a-scared o' nothin', an' you surely ain't nothin' to be a-scared of."

He had no hat; his clothes were more worn and ragged than she had believed. His face was gaunt, his eyes hollow.

The man in the black hat said, "You said this lady was nothin' to be scared of. You should have been here a few minutes ago."

"I seen it. If you folks hadn't been around, he'd of killed her. Scant Luther would."

"Do you know him?"

"Know of him. He's downright mean."

Mary held out her hand to him. "I am Mary Breydon. Do you live around here?"

"No."

"I told you my name."

"I'm Wat." He hesitated a moment and added, "I'm Wat Tanner."

"We're just feeding the passengers. Would you like to join us?"

"Don't mind if I do." He paused, looked at his hands, and said, "I'd have to wash up."

She indicated the shelf on the wall of the station just around the corner from the door. There was a tin basin, a bucket of water, a bar of soap, and a roller towel. "Help yourself. Then come on in."

She turned to the man in the black hat. "You'd better have something, too."

He glanced at her, then away. "Later. I'll just set out here for a spell."

She went inside, followed by Wat. The stage driver was coming out, and he held the door for them, seeing Wat for the first time. "Howdy, son."

Belligerently, Wat said, "I ain't your son!"

Wilbur dropped to his heels, his face grave. He put up a hand to turn the boy for a better view of his face. "Why! Why sure enough you ain't! But I'd of swore you were somebody's son."

The boy glared. "Mister, you're just full of—!" Glancing around, he saw Mary Breydon standing close by. "I don't believe you've even got a son."

"You'll know him if you see him," Wilbur replied. "He'll be ridin' a grizzly bear. Wears big Mexican spurs an' a top hat." Wilbur walked on to the stage, checking the team's harness.

The heavy-set man emerged from the station holding out his hand. "Name's Cowan, ma'am. I d'clare, I never saw a prettier sight than you with that whip!"

Mary blushed. "I'm afraid I—"

"You did just the right thing; only you be careful now. I travel this route now and again, and that Luther is a mean, mean man. You haven't seen the last of him."

Wilbur swung up to the box and released the brake, lifting his whip in salute. "Be another stage through about daybreak."

He cracked his whip, and the team was off with a lunge. For just a moment, she stood watching the dust cloud and listening to the diminishing sound. That was it, then. She was committed. It was her last touch with whatever had been, and what awaited her must be of her own doing.

The man with the black hat got up from the step. "If it is all right with you, I'll eat now."

"Please do."

The door closed, then opened for Wat.

"Did you have enough to eat, Mr. Tanner?"

He glanced at her, hitched his pants, and said, "Ma'am, you don't have to mister me. I figure we're friends. You can call me Wat."

"Thank you, Wat. I'll do that."

He glanced over his shoulder, then asked, speaking softly, "Is *he* a friend of yours?"

"We've just met, but he's been very helpful."

"Ma'am, you sure are lucky! Do you know who that *is*? That's *Temple Boone!*"

"I'm afraid I have never heard of Temple Boone."

He was aghast. "Ma'am, where d'you all come from that you don't know Temple Boone? You ask anybody, Denver to Julesburg to Laramie, an' they'll tell you about Temple Boone! He scouted for the army, he rode shotgun on gold shipments, hunted buffalo, lived with the Injuns. He's done about all a man can do! Why I reckon he's killed a dozen men, maybe. Only them that needed killin', o' course."

"I'm afraid there's a lot I must learn, Wat." She put a hand on his shoulder. "Will you help me, Wat? You're an old-timer out here, and I'm just a tenderfoot."

"Ma'am, anybody who can horsewhip Scant Luther is no tenderfoot. I *seen* it! Why nobody ain't dared cross him! Nobody! Not until you came."

"Wat? It's getting late. Won't your folks be worried about you?"

There was a long silence. "I got no folks. Ain't nobody going to be worried about me, and I don't *need* anybody."

"Everybody needs somebody, Wat. I have Peg, but if you'll let me, I'll have you, too."

"I don't need nobody."

"I know you don't, Wat, but we do, Peg and I. We're all alone, and we are not as strong as you are. If you have no place to go, why not stay here with us? At least until you decide to move on?"

"Well—all right. I got to earn me enough to buy a horse. A man without a horse an' saddle—well, he ain't very much, ma'am."

The shadows were long, and the sun was gone. A small wind stirred the leaves, and she shivered, looking around. For just a moment, her thoughts turned homeward, back to Virginia and the plantation before the war. The great white house with its columns, the carriages pulling up before the door, her father greeting the guests—it was all gone, gone forever now.

From inside came a rattle of dishes; then a light glowed as a lamp was lighted.

The night air was cool, and as she looked back along the valley, she smelled the hay from the barns, heard the movements of the horses. . . .Was this to be her world now? Was all the rest really gone? Or would it be what she wanted if a time came to go back?

"That man," she said suddenly, "said he would come back?"

"Yes, ma'am. He'll do it, too. He's got to . . . or leave the country. He won't leave. He's got too much workin' for him."

"What do you mean, Wat?"

"Oh . . . nothin'. Just seems him bein' around so long, with his friends and all. I just figured he'd not want to leave."

It was not at all what he had been thinking. He had something else in mind when he first spoke, she was sure of that. What did Scant Luther have "workin' for him"?

"Wat? Why don't you go in and help the girls clean up?"

"No, ma'am."

"No? Why, Wat, I thought—"

"No, ma'am. I'll do chores. I'll fetch wood or water. I'll feed the stock. I'll muck out behind the horses, but I won't do woman's work. I got my pride, ma'am. I batched some, doin' my own cookin', washin', and the like, but that's different."

" 'Batched'?"

"Yes, ma'am. That's what they call it when a man lives by

hisself and does for hisself. Like when he's a bachelor, they call it batching."

"I see. I guess I have a lot to learn, Wat."

"I'll help, ma'am." He gestured around. "I never worked in such a place, but I've been around stock all my life. I can hitch a team, if need be, or saddle a horse or herd cattle. I can carry messages a-horseback, grease wheels, and I don't mind fetchin' an' carryin'."

Temple Boone was lingering over his coffee when she went in, and he glanced from her to Wat, a faint, half-hidden smile in his eyes.

"Found you a man, I see."

She smiled. "Yes, it seems I have. He's going to stay on and help."

Her first thought had been for Peg and herself to sleep in the small cottage intended for them, but the more she considered it, the less the idea appealed to her. It would mean leaving Matty alone in the station, and it would be better if they were all together. She had her husband's rifle, and it was loaded. As a child, with her father, she had often hunted ducks or geese along the river, and she could shoot.

"I wish we had a gun for you, too, Matty."

"It would be better, mum, but there's never a house without its weapons. There's the butcher knife yonder and sticks of stove wood, lids from the stove, and there's pepper in the shaker. As for that, we could keep some water hot. Boilin' water has a way of changin' men's minds. We will have to do with what we have, mum."

Hands on her hips, she looked around. "We could take a bit of that clothesline and stretch it across the door not quite so high as a man's knee. When they come in an' trip, we could take the firewood to them or the poker from the fireplace."

"You might kill one of them!"

"Yes, mum, but when a body comes in your home of a night, breakin' in or sneakin' in without permission, he's takin' his own chances."

"You're right, Matty. Just for luck, we'll keep some water boiling, too."

"Yes, mum. Many's the man was killed before ever gun was

invented, an' not havin' a gun never stopped anybody from killin' who was a mind to. Nor a woman, either."

Temple Boone, sipping his coffee in silence, had said nothing. "Doesn't look like you're goin' to need me," he commented.

"We didn't know you were going to help."

"I sort of had it in mind, but maybe I'll just set around and watch the fun. The trouble is, you may have roped the wrong calf."

"What do you mean?"

"Supposin' Scant Luther pays you no mind at all? He doesn't have to come near you to put you out of business. This here station is your responsibility, so what if he just drives off your horses? Or sets fire to your hay?"

"Scant Luther is no fool. He can get himself hung bothering a woman, and he knows it. He might even do that, but if he does, he'll have it happen when nobody is around to see and when he can make it look like Injuns done it or something."

Of course, Temple Boone was right. Mary's immediate thought had been that he would want to strike back at her personally, but if she were hidden in the house, awaiting an attack, he could do whatever he wished outside.

"Thank you, Mr. Boone. You are right. We are short of weapons here, but—"

"Mum? I do have a pistol. It ain't much for size, but it's a comfort to have about."

"Better leave the barn and corrals to me," Boone suggested. "I'm not going anywhere, and I have a horse out there, too."

"I cannot ask you to do that, Mr. Boone. You might be killed."

"There isn't much a man can do west of the Mississippi where he might not get killed, ma'am. I've seen men gored by steers, killed in stampedes, thrown from buckin' horses, an' dragged with a foot caught in a stirrup.

"A man can fall off a cliff, have a boulder or a tree drop on him, or his mine tunnel can cave in on him. There's a hundred ways a man can get himself killed out here that has nothing to do with guns or Injuns or outlaws. It's a rough country, ma'am."

"But this is my problem."

"Mine, too. I'll be sleepin' out there, and folks prowlin' in the night worry me some."

"You'll make enemies."

"I've had a few here and there. Enemies are good for a man. Keeps him from gettin' careless with himself."

When he had stepped outside, Mary closed the door and dropped the bar in place. She went to the table and sat down. Matty brought her some food and a pot of coffee. "Better eat, mum. It's going to be a long night."

"Yes, of course. Where's Peg?"

"She was tired, so I made up a bed from the things you brought on the stage. She's fast asleep."

"Who is he, Matty?"

"Temple Boone? Don't you be thinkin' about him, ma'am. He's one of those who are just here, there, and around. He'll drift, and you'll see no more of him."

"He's a strange man."

"That he is."

She was tired. Hungry though she was, it was an effort to eat. She turned the wick down so the lamp gave off only a feeble glow. Then she went into the room where Peg lay sleeping and lay down beside her.

Tomorrow there would be much to do. First to clean up the mess Luther had left behind, then to organize some efficient procedure for handling the stages, feeding the passengers, and getting them on the road again. She wished she could visit some of the other stations along the Cherokee Trail to see how they were doing it.

In the darkness, the man called Boone was only another shadow in a maze of shadows cast by the barn, the corral, the house across the road. The only sounds came from the horses, and his senses isolated their vague sounds from the others, leaving a vacant place where strange sounds could register. Near a corner of the corral where the shadows were deepest, he sat on the ground, the rifle stock on the earth between his legs, the barrel leaning against his shoulder.

And then, for a long time, there was only stillness, with the wind moving, a soft wind, barely stirring the leaves, a wind so light that its stirring left a place for the faint sounds of a man moving.

Inside the house, there was only a dim, reddish glow from the dying embers in the fireplace and a faint glow of light around the turned-down lamp. Outside, the leaves rustled, and Matty turned over on her cot dreaming of the sea rustling on the sands of Kerry.

Mary Breydon awakened suddenly. Her eyes flared open, but she lay still, unmoving, listening, every sense alert.

At first, there was no sound but the whisper from the kettle on the fire. From where she lay, she could see, in the faint glow from the turned-down lamp, the movement of the door latch. Ever so gently, it was lifted. There was a pressure on the door, which held firmly in place; then the latch eased down again.

Mary Breydon threw back the blankets and swung her feet to the floor, feeling for her slippers. She stood up, slipping into her robe.

What was it Matty had said? Anything was a weapon if you used it as such. Even if much of the water had boiled away, the teakettle should be half full, the coffeepot, also.

Somebody was trying to get in. Scant Luther? Perhaps. Or Temple Boone? After all, what did she know about him? Why had he stayed behind? Did he really wish to help or was he simply—

She waited, listening. How silly could she be? It was probably only Boone wanting a cup of coffee!

It must be cold out there, and he was keeping watch. If anyone came to the stage station, he would surely know. She glanced at the window. The shutters were closed. Walking to the fireplace, she added water to the kettle, then replaced the lid and edged it closer to the coals.

She thought about her rifle. If only it wasn't so long! What she needed was a handgun, something that could not be wrested from her hands. Still, if she could shoot fast enough—

Her husband had said he had heard of men firing a rifle from waist level, but could she? And be sure of hitting anything? Of course, at that distance—

She sat down at the table with her coffee, suddenly realizing what she had was cold coffee in a cold cup. How silly! She had forgotten to fill her own cup before putting fresh water in the coffee!

Why not go back to sleep? It had probably just been Boone. Anyway, nothing had happened, and she might have imagined it. No, she had not. She *had* seen the latch lift!

She was so tired, so very tired. Nobody could get in with that bar across the door, so why not go back to sleep?

Returning to the bedroom, she lay down again. From where she lay, the door was in view. Her eyes closed.

Outside in the darkness, the wind stirred, and dried leaves skittered across the hard-packed earth of the yard.

The man named Boone opened his eyes. He had not slept, only closing his eyes, resting a little, but his senses were alert. He heard nothing, yet he was uneasy, and he had learned to trust those feelings. Usually, they stemmed from some subconscious awareness his consciousness had not noted. Luther was a bitter, brutal man, not accustomed to being thwarted in any way. Careful to make no sound, Boone shifted his position, taking the rifle in his hands.

He looked toward the house. He would like a cup of coffee, but to go there now might frighten them, and that Irish girl had a pistol. He eased his belt gun into a better position and tightened his coat around him. It was chilly, mighty chilly. What had he gotten into this for, anyway? It was none of his business. If a woman wanted to come out here and take a job like that, she should expect trouble.

A very pretty woman, too. And a lady. Anybody could see that. Her way of looking at you, the way she gathered her skirts, the way she moved—

One of the horses blew softly, showing alarm. Boone took a fresh grip on his rifle and looked around carefully, searching every shadow. Some of those horses were broncs, wild stuff broken to drive. They were as alert as any wild animal would be.

Nothing . . . no sound, no—

It was just a whisper of sound, some coarse material brushing against something else. The corral bars? Perhaps.

Mentally, he swore. He was not in a good position for quick movement. To rise up now would make some sound, however small, and if it was Scant Luther come back, he would not be alone.

Then, so close it scared him, he heard a faint whisper. "She'll have the door barred."

"I say take the horses an' go. That's a good bunch of stock."

"Like hell! What d'you think I brought this whip along for? We're goin' in there! Hell, that bar don't mean nothin'! I lived here too long! I can get that bar out of the way! What d'you think I done the time Buck passed out in there? Him with the door barred? I got in, didn't I?"

"I don't like it, Scant. What about that Boone feller?"

"Aw, he's long gone! What would he stick around for?"

"Maybe he's gettin' sweet on her. He taken up for her, didn't he?"

They moved away, and Boone reached up, grasping one of the corral bars to pull himself erect. He had an urge to shoot, but beyond them was the house, and a bullet from his rifle would go through several inches of pine, and he might injure one of the women or that little girl. A man with a gun had not only to think of what he was shooting at but where the bullet might go if it missed, and almost any kind of a gun might carry up to a mile.

If he could just get across the corral and come up on their flank—

He rested a boot on the lower pole, then the next. Quickly, he threw himself over and landed on his feet on the soft earth inside. His boots made a soft *thump* as he landed.

A boot grated on gravel, and someone whispered hoarsely, "What was *that*?"

Luther's tone was impatient. "A horse, damn it! Just a horse stampin'!"

Like a ghost, Boone crossed the corral. They were at the house now. Luther said he could unbar the door from the outside. *How?*

There might be a crack in the door through which a stick or a stiff wire might be slipped to lift the bar. Of course, when it fell, it would make a sound, but they would be inside before there could be any reaction.

He hesitated. Should he take a chance and go over the corral bars? Or should he shoot from the partial protection of the corral? It was a little safety to be traded for increased mobility, and he wanted to go over. They would be doubly alert now. One of them thought he had heard something, and also, as they were nearing the house, their every sense would be alert.

Inside the house, Mary Breydon turned restlessly in her half sleep. Her robe, which she had kept on, had tightened around her legs, and irritated by it, she had half sat up to free herself from it when she heard a faint scratching from the door.

Instantly, she was on her feet, tightening her robe. The sound was coming from the door.

Frightened, she stepped into the room. What should she do? What *could* she do?

Suddenly, unbelievably, the bar seemed to lift of its own volition. It tipped back, then fell to the floor with a thump. Instantly, the latch lifted, and men plunged into the room. Turning swiftly, without thinking, she caught up the coffeepot and with one sweeping, swinging movement, threw the scalding coffee into their faces!

A man screamed as the scalding coffee struck and began pawing at his eyes as if he would tear them out. Another wheeled and plunged through the door, fighting to get out. At the door, he tripped and fell sprawling, and Scant Luther leaped over him to get into the room. Dropping the now-empty coffeepot, Mary grabbed up the broom but did not swing it. At the moment it came into her hands, she remembered something the major had told her long ago, and as Luther lunged to grab her, she thrust hard with the end of the broomstick.

The thrust caught him in the pit of the stomach, and he stopped, gasping for a breath. Swiftly, she struck again. Out of wind, his wild grasp at the broom failed, and he took a glancing blow to the face that ripped his cheek.

From outside, there was a shot, then another one. Luther scrambled for the door, and she struck him again, this time with the business end of the broom.

Matty appeared in her door, pistol in hand.

Mary Breydon stopped, staring after them, half sick with fright.

"They're gone, mum," Matty said. "You did 'em in."

From outside, there was a sound of running, then of horses charging away into the night.

Temple Boone appeared in the doorway, rifle in hand. He stepped inside, picking up the now-empty coffeepot. "Now ain't that hell? Just when I wanted a good cup of coffee!"

THREE

M ary awakened in the first gray light of day and lay still, staring up at the ceiling and trying to organize her day.

She had moved in and taken charge, and she had survived that and her first night. The word that she was a woman would by now have reached Mark Stacy, who was division agent, and running a stage station was no job for a lady. That would be his first thought. Yet she had taken charge, and she had fired Scant Luther. No man could have done it better.

Yet he would be coming soon, and what he must find was a better station. No, not a better one. It must be *the* best. It must be neat, clean, with good food ready to serve when the stages arrived.

The teams must be changed promptly, the barns must be clean, all the mess Scant Luther had left must be cleaned up.

How much time did she have? A day? Two days? She might even have a week. There were other stations, and Stacy was a busy man.

The station first, for here they would feed the passengers, handle the mail and any shipments there were, and that would be the first place Stacy would notice. Above all, good food, served hot, something passengers could go away talking about.

They had begun cleaning but had barely touched the work to be done. That needed to go forward.

Next, an inventory of what supplies were on hand and what was needed. A careful check of the stables to see what needed to be done. At that moment, she thought of her father.

Sitting up in bed, she swung her feet to the floor, feeling for her slippers. "Thank God, papa," she whispered to herself, "you never had a son!"

He would have been shocked to hear her say it, but had there been a son, she would never have learned how to do so many things that now she knew. He had loved having her ride out with him in the morning, and she had learned how to handle horses, how to keep a stable, even how to use a whip.

"This will all be yours someday," her father had said, "and you'd better know how to run it. If the man you marry is no better than some of those I've seen coming around here, you will need to know.

"And, honey, you handle your own affairs yourself. Manage your own money. Let nobody else do it no matter how well they think they can handle it. Always keep your own money in your own hands!"

Luckily, Marshall had agreed. Even before they were married, he assured her, "Keep what's your own. Our children will have something to start with no matter what. I'll take care of you."

They had not planned for a war. They had not expected the lovely plantation to be devastated, the buildings burned, fences torn down, stock driven off by guerrillas.

She would check the supplies in the station storeroom, the tools, the harness, the horses, and the feed situation. In the kitchen, she sat down and made a list of things that would need doing. Only then did she bathe and dress.

When she returned to the kitchen, Matty had coffee on and was preparing breakfast. "I found some bacon, mum, and there's eggs."

"Matty? I don't want to frighten you, but keep your pistol where you can reach it."

"Yes, mum. I don't frighten easy, mum. I grew up with four big brothers and had to fight for it all until they were growed enough to respect me." She filled Mary's cup. "They were troubling times, mum, and there was many a time when I wished for a gun but had none."

There was a tap on the door, and when Matty opened it, Wat was there, and behind him, Temple Boone.

Mary hesitated, looking into her cup. It had to be done; she must ask them because she must have them. She could not do it all alone.

"Wat? Would you like to work for me? Here?"

"Yes, ma'am, as long as it's men's work."

"It is. The first thing will be to clean the stable."

"That's a mighty big job for one man," Boone protested. "I mean, the way Luther left it."

"I can do it." Wat looked up belligerently. "I'll want five dollars a month and found."

"Do a good job and I'll pay you ten." She lifted her eyes to Boone. "How about you? Are you looking for work?"

"No." He spoke quickly, and something seemed to give way inside her. She could not do it alone. The outside work would be too much. "But I promised myself I'd stay on and see you get settled. I might ride over to Bonner's. I hear tell there's been a man rustlin' work over there."

"Neither of you will probably want to help when you hear what I have planned." She paused again. "I want this job. I need this job. I've got to have this place in such shape by the time Mark Stacy gets here that he'll have no reason to discharge me."

"He's a reasonable man."

"Do you know him?"

"I do. He's a widower. No family. Eats, sleeps, and breathes this stage line."

"A young man?"

"Depends on where you start countin'. I'd say he's about forty. I'd say he's young enough to see that you're a mighty handsome woman."

She flushed and looked straight into his eyes. "I am not

thinking of that. However I may look is not going to help me one bit on this job. It will be what I do and how well I do."

"You're right about that. Stacy will see you're a pretty woman, but like I said, he lives this stage line. If you're not doin' the job, he wouldn't keep you on if you was Cleopatra."

"I would feel the same way, Mr. Boone. What I want to do is have this place spotless and working efficiently by the time he gets here."

She drank the last of her coffee. "Matty? Fix him some breakfast. He's going to work."

Boone started to speak, then turned toward the table. "You heard the lady, Matty. Breakfast it is."

Outside, the sun was bright. For a moment, she looked around. The cottage over there, that was where she was to live, but that could wait. The corrals, at least, were well built. She walked past them to the barn and hesitated at the door. It was literally a mess.

The earth floor was covered with old horse manure, with trampled hay and straw. It had not been cleaned in weeks, probably in months. There were no horses in the stalls. Frowning, she turned to look at the corrals.

Six horses . . . and she had a stage coming in this morning. She looked again. That was the team that had brought her into this station, and they should have more rest.

"What will I do with the manure, ma'am?"

Wat had come up beside her with a shovel whose handle was taller than he was.

"Put it out back of the barn for now, Wat. I may use some of the older material to fertilize a garden."

He looked at her. "A garden, ma'am?"

"Yes, Wat. If we are going to feed people here, we have no reason not to raise our own vegetables. At least, we can try."

Temple Boone was walking toward her. "I can help the boy," he offered.

"Mr. Boone? Shouldn't there be more horses? That's the team that brought us in last night. I assume they are fit to take a stage out again, but it would be better if they had more rest. And what if one of them was indisposed?"

He smiled at the word but looked thoughtful when he glanced

toward the corral. "There should be more horses here, ma'am. In fact, my horse should be here."

He paused, and glancing at him, she saw his eyes had lost the lurking smile. "You'd better let me handle this, ma'am. But you're right. There should be at least six more horses in that corral aside from mine. That Luther's been a lot of things, but I didn't think he was a horse thief."

"That's a very serious accusation."

"It is, ma'am, but a man who steals a man's horse can steal his life. Many a time a man's horse is all that's between him and a mighty ugly death. We don't have much patience with horse thieves, ma'am."

"The law—"

"Ma'am, I respect the law. We need it, but we don't have any more protection than we can give ourselves. There ain't an officer of any kind within a hundred miles, and even if they were around, they can't act until after the fact, ma'am. After your horse is stole or you're dead, they can hunt down those who done it, but you're just as dead as if there was no law. Any man who steals my horse has bought hisself a ticket."

She was thinking, frowning a little. "Mr. Boone? Do you think Scant Luther would steal from Ben Holladay?"

"He'd be careful, mighty careful. Ben's not a man to fool around with, and Scant's not one to take chances."

"What facts do we have, Mr. Boone? Six horses, seven, including yours, are missing. You say Scant is no fool, so where are the horses?

"Suppose," she suggested, "he planned to steal them but did not want to take chances? What would he do?"

Boone pushed his hat back on his head. "Well—I reckon he might just drive those horses off, not too far, mind you, an' hold them where he could produce them if need be. Then he might wait to see what happened."

"And where would he hold them?"

Temple Boone looked off down the valley, thinking. After a moment, he said, "This here's pretty wide-open country. There's canyons here and there, some good hideaways if you know the country, but I'd say the best place would be Steamboat Rock, but that's quite a ways."

"Wouldn't there be tracks?"

Boone hesitated. "Could be. Ain't been much rain lately."

"Are you a good tracker, Mr. Boone? I understood you'd been a scout for the army?"

"Now see here! What're you thinkin' about?"

"I'm going after those horses, Mr. Boone. I am the agent for the company, and I am responsible."

"Ma'am, you're crazy! Off in those hills, alone, that Luther would shoot you down like a dog! You just back off now. You leave this to me."

She turned swiftly away without replying and walked back to the house. Once inside the station, she stood thinking; then she turned to helping Matty prepare for the incoming stage.

"Matty? I don't know who is on the next stage, but we have to feed them, and Matty, I want to send them away from here talking about it." She looked around at Matty. "Are you a fighter, Matty?"

"I'm Irish, mum."

"All right, we're fighting for your job and mine. Let's win."

When the stage rolled in, the food was on the table, and it was hot. There had been little to choose from, for she had yet to order supplies, but there was ham and beans and two apple pies made from dried apples.

Among the supplies, she found some bolts of calico for trading with the Indians. From one of them, she cut enough material for a tablecloth. It was bright red, but it was also attractive.

There were six passengers, one of them a woman; the others were city men and one army officer headed for Fort Laramie.

One of the city men, a tall, serious-looking man with a beard, paused in leaving, hat in hand. "Thank you, ma'am. That's the best food we've had on the trip."

"Thank you, sir. Come back next week when I've had a chance to order supplies."

He smiled. "I'll do that, ma'am. I really will."

When the stage was gone, she took off her apron. "Matty? You're in charge. I'll be gone for a few hours."

"Hours?"

"I've got a job to do, Matty. Some of our horses are missing."

"What—?"

"Ma'am?" Wat interrupted Matty. "I can track."

"*You* can?"

"I growed up out here, ma'am. I been trackin' lost cows or findin' hid calves since I was able to walk. Anyway, I figure I know where those horses are."

For a moment, she hesitated. "All right, Wat. Get our horses—Oh, I forgot! We don't have any horses but those from the stage that just came in."

"Can you walk a couple of miles?" Wat asked. "It ain't no further."

"All right, Wat. Shall we go?"

He hesitated. "There's liable to be somebody there, an' I think we'd better have a gun."

"I'll get my rifle."

"No, ma'am. There's a shotgun in there. It's a spare for the express messenger. I seen it, and I seen some loads for it. You take your rifle and they ain't goin' to pay much attention, but you take that shotgun an' get close—they'll listen to you, ma'am."

She looked at him again and hesitated. She was a fool, and Mr. Boone was right. She would be more than a fool if she went after those horses with nothing but a small boy to show her the way. Nevertheless—

Her jaw muscles tightened. She would go. If a man could do it, why couldn't she?

Wat led the way, taking off down a narrow, dusty path back of the corral that led off across the road and under the trees. When they had walked almost a mile, Wat dropped back beside her. "Ma'am? If you want to say somethin' to me now, you *hsst* at me. Don't you go to speakin' out. They'll hear you, sure."

"What's there, Wat? Do you know?"

"Yes'm. It's just a rope corral an' a place under the trees where they bed down. There's water there, an' stole horses been held there many a time."

It was very quiet. A fly buzzed past her face. She felt a small trickle of perspiration on her cheek. She brushed it away and shifted the shotgun again. It was heavy, heavier than she thought.

Wat stopped again, then motioned her forward, and she saw them. There were nine horses in a small rope corral, and beyond them, under a tree, a man was sleeping on his rolled-out bed. Nearby, there were some ashes and a coffeepot on the fire. As she started to step forward, Wat put up a restraining hand.

Another man came down from the trees, and walking over to the bed, he bent over to pick up his gun belt. Quickly, she stepped out into the open. "Leave that alone!"

Startled, the man paused and looked around. He saw only a woman and a small boy. He spoke. "Bob?"

"Lemme alone. I'm sleepin'."

"Bob, we got comp'ny."

The man sat up. "Huh? What—" He looked again. "Hell, it's that woman from the stage station. The one who took the whip to Scant."

"That's right, gentlemen, and I've come for the stage-company horses and also that saddle horse that belongs to Temple Boone."

"To *who*?" The seated man got quickly to his feet. "Damn it, Pike! You never told me that was Boone's horse!"

"What dif'rence does it make? Who the hell is Boone?"

"If he finds we got his horse, you'll sure be findin' out who he is." He turned toward Mary Breydon, who had walked closer.

"Lady," he started to say.

"Back up and sit down again. You, too, Pike."

"Now, look here, ma'am," Pike started to say, "I—"

"Mr. Pike, or whatever your name is, I've got an express gun here, it is loaded, and I'm very nervous. If you should frighten me, I am apt to shoot it, and I have done a lot of shooting at ducks. I think it would be much easier to hit you. I hope I don't have to."

She gestured with a movement of her head. "Wat, get our horses."

"Like hell!" Pike started to take a step, and her thumb eared back the hammer on one barrel. It was a sharp, very audible click. Pike stopped so quick he teetered on his toes, then settled back.

"For God's sake, Pike!" Bob said. "She *means* it!"

Wat was running a lead rope from halter to halter with all the skill of an old-timer. Then he caught a mane hold on one of the stage horses and swung to its back.

"Kid," Pike shouted, "you get off that hoss an' leave them be or by the eternal I'll have your hide!"

"You got to catch me first!" Wat yelled. "Come on, ma'am! Give 'em a barrel just for luck!"

"Not this time." She was very cool. "Stay away from Cherokee Station," she said quietly, amazed at her own steadiness. "I don't want to kill a man again."

Only when she was under the trees did she turn her back to them, and behind her she heard Bob say, "Did you hear that? She said she didn't want to kill a man *again!*"

Wat looked down from his horse. "Who'd you kill, ma'am? Was it one of them sojers who tore up your plantation?"

"I have never killed anyone, Wat. I don't know why I said 'again.' It just slipped out."

"It was the right word, ma'am. You surely gave 'em the right word." He began to chuckle. "Wait until Scant Luther hears about this!"

FOUR

She remembered so well what her father had said, "Don't waste time worrying about the mistakes of yesterday. Each morning is a beginning. Start from there."

As she had begun, so she continued. Each night, before going to bed, she took a small tablet and planned her work for the next day, thinking out each step that must be taken.

Wat, working like a man twice his size, had cleaned the stable. She walked through it, inspecting the job he had done. When she finished, she said, "Wat? Come back to the station with me."

At the station, she said, "Matty? There was a piece of that apple pie left. Is it still there?"

"Yes, mum."

"Give it to Wat. Let him eat it now. He's just finished a job he can be proud of."

As she was leaving the station, she turned to him again. "Wat? Can you whittle?"

"Whittle? Ma'am, any boy who has a jackknife can whittle. I been whittlin' since . . . well, I been whittlin' seems like forever."

"All right, in your spare time, or whenever you feel like it, I want you to whittle some pegs about a foot long, about an inch thick, and I want them peeled."

"How many?"

"About two dozen, I think." At his puzzled expression, she said, "I want some pegs on which to hang the harness in the tack room."

"You could use nails. That's what most folks do."

"Wooden pegs are better, Wat. They are less destructive of the harness."

"All right, ma'am. I'll sure do it." He turned back to the table and the slice of apple pie.

When Wilbur Pattishal wheeled his stage into the street of Laporte, Mark Stacy was waiting for him on the boardwalk in front of the stage.

"Wilbur? What's this I hear? Who's that woman running the station out at Cherokee?"

Wilbur's face was expressionless. Only his eyes showed a faint amusement. "You hired M. O. Breydon. That's her."

"A *woman*? At Cherokee?"

"She fired Scant Luther," Wilbur said. "And man, did she ever fire him! Ran him out o' there with a whip!"

"Scant? I don't believe it."

"She done it, though. And that ain't all. Somebody—I ain't sayin' it was Scant—stole a team and Temple Boone's gelding. She went over there afoot an' brought 'em back. She had herself a shotgun, and the way Wat tells it, they didn't see fit to put up any argument."

"Who is Wat?"

"Youngster she has workin' for her. She's got an Irish maid, too. Maid an' cook."

"We'll see about that. I gave nobody authority to do any hiring. And a woman? At Cherokee?"

"Mr. Stacy? Was I you, I'd walk soft goin' out there. You go in there all hot to change things an' you're liable to lose her.

"She taken over just about the time you left for Kansas City, and in the two weeks she's been there, she's turned that place around. You go out there an' take a good long look at things before you start firin' people."

Stacy swore softly, but he was thoughtful. Wilbur Pattishal was a character, no question about that, but he was also the best driver on the line, and he was no fool.

Fired Scant Luther? Impossible! Nonetheless, operating a stage station was no job for a woman no matter how big and tough she was.

Fired Scant? There had to be something wrong about that. Could be they were working together. There was no question that Scant was a thief, but nobody was in a hurry to accuse him of it.

He had started into the office; now he stopped. She had recovered Temple Boone's horse. What was Boone doing out there?

Mark Stacy knew Boone but slightly. He had come drifting into the country very much a loner and supposedly from Texas. Like many another western man, his past was his own secret, and he never spoke of it. He had worked for other stage lines as a shotgun guard, had trapped some, prospected, rounded up and captured wild horses, and the story around was that he was good with a gun.

What was he doing at Cherokee?

When Wilbur came out of the office, Stacy turned to him. "Wilbur? What's Boone doing out there? Is he tied in with Luther?"

"The other way around, seems to me. He was on the stage Miz Breydon come in on, settin' back there quiet, mindin' his own affairs.

"He seen her fire Luther, standin' by, just lookin' on, but I had an idea if she'd needed help, he'd have stepped in mighty quick." Wilbur chuckled. "Only she didn't need help. No way."

"I don't like it, Wilbur. D'you suppose there was some connection between them before?"

Pattishal took out a thin cigar and bit off the end. "If I was you, I'd not waste time speculatin'. I'd go out there an' see for myself. But I'd step mighty soft if I was you, too. That's no ordinary woman. That's a *lady*."

Stacy snorted and walked off down the street. What a mess! Getting rid of Luther was one thing, and he was glad the man was gone, but a *woman*? At Cherokee, of all places?

When he reached the corner, he paused. A big man standing on the corner turned toward him. The man wore a badge on his shirt. "Howdy, Mark! Hear you got a woman runnin' the station out to Cherokee?"

"Not for long. That's no place for a woman no matter how tough she is." Stacy paused. "Marshal? Have you heard anything new about Denver Cross's outfit?"

The marshal was watching a rider down the street, and he took his time replying. "No, not a word." He turned his eyes to Stacy. "But I'd be careful if you're shipping any treasure. They are around somewhere, holed up back in the mountains."

"How about Johnny Havalik?"

"There's a story around; some of the boys been telling it in the saloons. The word is that Johnny's dead. The story is that Denver Cross shot him."

"I wish it had been the other way around. Havalik seemed like the best of a bad lot."

"He was a loner, though, and Cross wanted men around who would step to his music. He didn't like loners."

"You don't know where they're holed up?"

"No, I don't, and I'm not lookin'. I've trouble enough right here in Laporte and between here and Denver. What happens north of here—

"The fact is, I've had an idea there was some kind of tie-up between Scant Luther and Cross. I was keepin' an eye on Scant, hoping something would turn up, but now that woman of yours turned him out, so I've lost that chance."

"Luther and Cross? How did you make that tie-up?"

"Cross used to waste around down to Fort Griffin. So did Luther. Scant had a saloon down that way where some of the rough crowd used to hang out, and Denver dealt cards there for a while."

There had been no time to dream, no time to remember. Only at night, when at last she could lie down, could she think back to other days. Yet they were now no more than a memory, almost as if they had never been. The great white house with the pillars, the long green fields, the white fences, the splendid horses, and the long, quiet rides with her father as he rode over and supervised the plantation.

All gone now. The land was there, and the land was hers, and sometime after the war was over, she would go back; she would rebuild the house, the barns, the fences. Not as magnificently as they had been, for she would not have the money, but she would rebuild and begin again.

That was all for tomorrow. Perhaps before Peg became a young lady, if they were fortunate. Possibly she, too, could come of age in the beautiful land now so torn and ravaged by war, that land so far away, so lost to her now.

"One day," her father had often said, "this will all be yours, so you must learn how it functions. Never trust your affairs to anyone else. If you have a foreman or a superintendent, that's fine, but be sure you know what is going on. You give the orders, you check to make sure your wishes are carried out."

The old days were far away now, but the lessons were not. Here the problems were the same, increased by the difficulty that some men simply did not like to take orders from a woman.

Her every muscle ached. Working right along with Matty, she had washed, swept, mopped, and dusted. They had baked bread, made cookies, and she had made up a requisition for supplies.

At last, she had turned to the cottage where they would live. When it was swept and mopped, she moved their bedding there, put her few books on a shelf, and got out the picture of her late husband.

Shortly before stage time, when they were setting the table, she suddenly thought of something.

"Matty? At first, you did not tell me you had a pistol."

"No, mum, not at first. A woman's not expected to have a gun."

"But you had one?"

"Yes, mum, and I kept it hid. You'd best do the same. If they know you have it, they will do their best to get it from you. If they don't know you have it until you need one, it can make all the difference."

It was good advice, and she must have a pistol, a gun she could handle easily and have close at all times. She remembered the shock when she first looked into Scant Luther's eyes and saw the hatred and the violence there. He was a man who would stop at nothing, and the story that he had been horse-whipped by a woman would by now have reached from Denver to Laramie to Julesburg.

The passengers were boarding the stage when Wilbur Pattishal stopped near her. "Ma'am? Mark Stacy will be on the stage next time it comes. Or maybe the time after, but he's comin', and he doesn't believe any woman can run a stage station on the Cherokee Trail."

"Thank you, Wilbur. We're ready for him."

"I'd sure hate to lose you, ma'am. All the people are sayin' how good your food is and all. It's the best I ever et." He paused. "Seen some Injuns this side of Virginia Dale. Friend-lies, seemed like, but Injuns are notional, ma'am, so you be careful. Remember this, an Injun respects strength an' mighty little else. He respects strength an' honesty."

"I have heard you could trust their word."

"Ma'am," Wilbur said patiently, "Injuns are folks. They're like you an' me and Scant Luther. Some you can trust; some you can't. There's just as many honest folks among Injuns as among white or black. An' there's just as many thieves and liars.

"Injuns have their decent men like Mark Stacy, an' they have their Scant Luthers, too. There's just no way a body can say anybody is all this or that. You've got to judge each man by himself."

"Thank you, Wilbur."

She watched the stage leave and then turned back toward the stage station. Wat was washing his hands in the basin by the door. She stopped near him.

"Wat? I want to thank you. No matter what happens here, I shall never forget you. You've been a pillar of strength, and no man could have done better."

He flushed and turned his face away. "Thanks, ma'am. It was an awful mess when you taken over."

"Wat? Did you ever go to school?"

"No, ma'am, not exactly. We lived near a preacher one time, an' he taught some of us who lived around to read an' write.

"Johnny, he used to bring me books once in a while. I never did see him more'n three or four times, but he brought me a book or two. I read them."

"What books, Wat?"

"*Ivanhoe* was one, and then there was *Robinson Crusoe*. I surely did like them books. It taken me a while to read them, but 'twas worth it."

"Who was Johnny?"

The expression left his face. "Just a feller we knew. He was just a rider-by. Stopped in now an' again."

"Did you live on a ranch?"

"Sort of. Pa didn't have money for many cows. He done what he could."

"Where was this, Wat?"

"Edge of the mountains. That was the last one. We had us two, three places. One was back in Kansas somewheres. Injuns burned us out, run off the stock. Pa worked in a store for a while. When that job played out, he tended bar in a saloon in Wichita."

"You moved a lot."

"Yes, ma'am. Pa was a mover. He wanted a place of his own. Didn't do him much good when he got it."

"Where was that?"

"Edge of the mountains." Wat dried his hands. "All right if I eat now, ma'am?"

At her nod, he turned quickly away and went inside, and she looked after him, frowning with irritation. She had learned exactly nothing except that he had once lived in Kansas and that he had read *Ivanhoe* and *Robinson Crusoe*.

Later, she asked, "Did you have many books in your home, Wat?"

"No, ma'am." He glanced at her, embarrassed. "Pa never learned to read." Then, defensively, he said, "We had us a

Bible, a great big old book. Pa said it had been in the family more'n a hundred years.

"There was a lot of writing in the back of it, names an' dates an' such. Pa set store by it. Said all the births an' deaths was written in it."

"You should have that Bible, Wat. It is probably a family record."

"Yes, ma'am."

"Where is it now?"

"Up there. Edge of the mountains, I guess."

From outside, there was a pound of hoofs, and when she stepped outside, she saw Temple Boone.

"Ma'am," he warned, "Mark Stacy's on the stage. He'll be here within the hour!"

FIVE

For a moment, she stood irresolute. This was the moment she had feared. Stacy had been shocked to hear that a woman had taken over Cherokee Station. He was prepared, so the rumors were, to discharge her and bring in a man, almost any man.

"Mum? We're fighters, you know, but on occasion we are bluffers, too. He's expectin' a woman, so give him a woman!"

"What?" Puzzled, she turned to look at Matty.

"You're not only a woman, mum, you're a lady, and a beautiful one with it. He's lookin' to find a woman—the Good Lord only knows what manner of woman he's expectin'—but not you, mum.

"Go quickly now and change! Put on the blue dress; it's that beautiful no man could withstand it! Put on the blue dress and be a-waitin' him! He's expectin' a woman, so give him a lady, a grand lady! All in a lovely gown and all! He'll be speechless, mum!

"If it is a fight we're in, I say come out a-fightin' with your best weapons! Me old father used to say, 'Never let 'em get set! Take 'em off their feet an' keep 'em so!' It's you, mum, must do

it! Be the great lady you are and he'll never have the nerve to
fire you! Before he gets his wits about him, he'll be on the
stage an' gone!"

For a moment, she just stared. Of course! Matty was right,
so right!

"All right! But you, too! You were a maid once, you said.
You told me you'd the black dress and the apron left, but that
isn't what we want! Just a fresh dress and an apron! Quickly
now! And you, too, Peg! Come! We've only minutes!"

She ran into the other room of the cottage and changed. Her
hair, it looked a fright. Still—she took her brush and comb,
looked a moment, and made swift touches here and there.

Her dress was lovely. Fortunately, she'd taken it out for
Matty to press only the other day, and it had been hanging
ready—ready for what?

She had barely crossed to the station when they heard a
shout and the rattling of chains, the pounding of hoofs. The
stage swept up, turned in a cloud of dust, and the weary
passengers began to descend.

She went out on the steps and stood waiting. The passengers
started toward the steps, then stopped. "Gentlemen? And ladies?
Welcome to Cherokee Station!" Gracefully, she stepped to one
side. "If you will come in, please?"

Staring, they paraded past her, two women and four men.
And then at last the man she knew at once was Mark Stacy.

He was tall, strongly built, not at all bad-looking. He had
stepped down from the stage without seeing her and was
talking for a moment with the driver. As he turned away, the
fresh team was led out by Temple Boone, and as they passed
him, he looked up to see Mary Breydon.

He stopped, his mouth open. Hastily, he gulped, closed his
mouth, and, confused, started toward her. He had been expecting a termagant, one of those big, strong women, as forceful as
any man, such as one often found in western mining camps.
Instead, there was this utterly beautiful young woman.

A lady, they had said, and so she obviously was. Confused—
all his carefully chosen words were forgotten.

She smiled beautifully, graciously. "Mr. Mark Stacy, is it?

Welcome to Cherokee Station! Please come inside. Your food will grow cold.

"Peg? Will you show Mr. Stacy to his place? Please do."

Mark Stacy fumbled his way to his seat. The table was covered with a red calico cloth. There were red calico curtains at the windows, the floor was spotless, and the food smelled terrific. He glanced around.

It was like a different place. Only the old fireplace and the stove that had been added later to give greater warmth, only they were familiar. The windows were in all the right places, but the place itself . . . he couldn't believe it.

Mary sat down opposite him. She passed the plate, heaping with steaks. "It is buffalo steak, and many prefer it to beef. You're familiar with it, Mr. Stacy?"

"I was a buffalo hunter," he explained, "although I never ate a buffalo steak that tasted quite this good."

"They are a feature of Cherokee Station, Mr. Stacy. The meat of the country, you know!"

Mark Stacy was confused and somewhat irritated. He had a feeling of being taken advantage of but could not quite see how it was done. Certainly, no station on his or any stage line had either meals like this or a station manager as glamorous. It was nothing like what he had expected, and he did not quite know what to do about it.

"I must say, Miss—?" He was a thin man with a beard.

"It is Mrs. Breydon, sir. I regret to say I am a widow."

"What I wanted to say was that I've never had food like this on any stage line. Nor a station as attractive. I almost wish I could stop over."

"We haven't the facilities for that, sir, but one day we might. When we do, I hope you come this way again."

The stage driver thrust his head in the door. "Five minutes, folks!" The driver turned toward Stacy. "Will you be goin' on with us, Mr. Stacy?"

"I'll catch the next stage. I've some business here." He got up hastily and went out.

The driver was about to swing aboard. "She's a looker, ain't she, boss?"

"She is a handsome woman. Whether she's a station agent remains to be seen."

"Wait'll you see the barn. She's got it fixed like one o' them fancy private stables back East. Anything you want, it's right there, under your hand. She ain't missed a trick."

Stacy stood, hands on his hips, watching the stage roll out; then he walked to the stable.

Wooden pegs in the walls, extra harness all hung, collars on one peg, the rest of the harness on another. The stalls were clean, the tack room free of dust, the harness repair tools all laid out.

Had she known he was coming? Of course, she had. The grapevine always carried such news, and anyone who fed as well as she did was sure to have made friends along the line. Yet, even so, he had never seen a station so clean, so well organized, and she had been here less than three weeks. All this could not have been done in the few hours before his arrival.

He walked back to the door and surveyed the station. What had that passenger said? That he wished he could stop over?

The station itself, the corrals, the barn, and the cottage. It was a nice setup, nicely laid out, but he had not really noticed that when Luther was running the place. Woman or not, she had certainly improved the place, but how in God's world had she been able to fire Scant Luther?

He had planned to do it himself if Major Breydon did not succeed, and he had not looked forward to it. Surely, there would have been a physical encounter.

Another thought came to him. What was Boone doing here? He had led out the team, then disappeared. And that boy she had hired? What was his name?

He was not himself doubtful that a woman could run a stage station. He was doubtful that she could command the respect of the men she would need to hire and serve. Or handle outlaws—

That was another thing. Where was Denver Cross? If he was hid out somewhere in the area, he must be planning a move against the stages. What else was there? And soon gold shipments would be coming down from the mountains. And why was Temple Boone here?

He glanced toward the station, seeing a flash of blue when Mary Breydon passed the window. He felt a sudden surge of jealousy.

Of course. He'd been a fool. Boone was here because Mary Breydon was. If he kept her on, every loose drifter in the country as well as some of the others would be stopping by. Slowly, thinking the while, he walked back to the station.

"A cup of coffee, Mr. Stacy?"

He glanced at her, then nodded. "By the way, have you met Preston Collier yet?"

"Collier? No, I don't believe I have. Who is he?"

"He's a rancher, about the largest ranch in the area, I believe. They've a lovely home just over the hill a few miles. He runs a good many horses, and we've bought from him a time or two. He's a good man. Easterner. New York, I believe."

He sipped his coffee. "You know, Mrs. Breydon, I hired your husband, M. O. Breydon, not you."

"My husband was killed on the way West. Our initials were the same. I needed the job, and I believed I could do it. Now I am sure I can."

"You seem to have taken hold very well. Might I ask what your background is?"

"My father operated a rather large plantation. We had a good many horses, carriages of several kinds, and we entertained a lot. As my father had no son, he tried to teach me how to carry on."

"I see. You know this is Indian country?"

"I do."

"And there are outlaws."

"So I understand."

"What would you do if you were attacked?"

"What have the others done before me?"

"They defended themselves. Several were wounded or killed."

"And you lost some stock?"

"Of course. It is the horses Indians want most of all."

"I have a Henry rifle, Mr. Stacy. As for losing stock, a theft has already been attempted. I recovered the stock. I don't believe you have a man who could have done it better."

"Perhaps not. But a woman of your quality—"

"I am a woman who needs a job, Mr. Stacy. We are not talking of quality now, nor really are we talking of the fact that I am a woman. What we are both talking about is the question in your mind: can I do the job?

"I think I can do it. I have made a beginning. I suggest, sir, you give me time. As for Indians or outlaws, you yourself said some of your men had been wounded or killed. I am prepared to take that risk."

He stared into his coffee. What kind of a mess was this, anyway? He had thought to come down here, tell the woman quietly that it just wouldn't work, and then get somebody else, but he had not expected to find the station in such excellent shape, nor had he expected this kind of a woman.

Before he could speak, she said, "I doubt if you have had the time to check my list of supplies. There are several items not usually requested.

"I have asked for vegetable seeds and potatoes for planting. If we are to feed a large number of people here, I see no reason why we should buy vegetables when we can grow them right out here back of the station.

"I want to put in a garden, plant potatoes, carrots, onions, cabbage, Indian corn, and a few other things. I believe that I can cut the food bill by at least a third."

"It is a thought. By the way, where did you get the buffalo steaks?"

"Mr. Boone killed a buffalo. He was kind enough to bring us the meat."

"Ah, yes. Temple Boone. I observed that it was he who brought out the team. Have you taken it upon yourself to employ him, too?"

"I have not. Mr. Boone merely wished to help. Of course, he is employed by the stage line. That he had not told me until today."

"Temple Boone? Employed by us?"

"Yes, of course. He told me he had been hired by Ben

Holladay to catch and break or trade for horses from the Indians, horses for the stage lines."

Mentally, Stacy swore. Why hadn't he been told? Of course, why should he be told? The procurement of horses was not necessarily his responsibility, and such horses might be used anywhere along the line from Missouri to California.

"He should be a good man for the job. I understand he's had a lot of experience with wild stock."

Mary got up and moved away, and Stacy watched her talking with the Irish girl, then with her daughter. Slowly, sipping his coffee, he began to relax. He liked the smell of cooking, of coffee, and the quiet sounds of the women moving about.

A boy came in and sat down at the table, and the little girl brought him a plate with some cookies on it.

"Mrs. Breydon? May I speak with you a minute?"

"Please call me Mary, Mr. Stacy. All my friends do."

"I must warn you. Somewhere around here some outlaws have found a hideout. We do not know where it is, but we know who some of them are. I want you and all our agents to be aware of them, and they are no common run of outlaw. One of them is a man known as Denver Cross."

"You believe he will try to steal our horses?"

"I do not. Denver plays for bigger stakes, and I believe he is getting settled to wait for a gold shipment.

"There's mining in the mountains now. They've found gold along Cherry Creek and at several other points. Soon there will be a shipment going over our line to the East. I believe that is why Denver Cross is here."

"We will be careful."

SIX

She awakened to a rumble of thunder. For a moment, she lay still. The room was dark, but she knew that daylight was not far off. Slipping from her bed and careful not to awaken Peg, she donned her robe and slippers, then went quietly into the cottage living room and looked across at the station.

There was a light showing from the window and, to her surprise, a saddled horse at the hitching rail outside. Waiting for a distant flash of lightning, she glimpsed the horse, but it was unfamiliar.

At this hour?

Hurriedly, she returned to her room and dressed. For a moment, she hesitated. She still did not have a pistol, and she would look foolish crossing the road in the rain carrying a Henry rifle. Yet, suppose—?

There was a swift dash of rain, then a steady downpour. Taking up a thick Indian blanket, she held it over her head and around her shoulders; then, stepping out on the porch, she closed the door behind her and walked swiftly across the road to the station.

Shaking the drops from the blanket, she glanced toward the

barn. The door was open a few inches. On these chilly nights, that door was always closed and only opened to lead out the teams. It might be opened a little to let a man in or out but not just a crack. Somebody was probably watching from the barn. Wat Tanner slept in the tack room. Turning away, she opened the door to the station and stepped in.

The man at the long table turned sharply toward the door, his hand going to the opening of his coat; then, seeing a woman, he let the hand fall.

He was a strong but rough-looking man, his hat pushed back to reveal a swarthy, almost brutal face with high cheekbones and a slight scar at the corner of his mouth that pulled the corner down somewhat. It was a face that once seen, would never be forgotten. And she had seen it before.

"Mum?" Matty's tone was even. "This gentleman's inquiring for a boy, a young lad."

The man's teeth flashed in a smile. "He was working for me, and he ran away. I've come to take him back."

She folded the blanket and placed it on the end of the bench. "What if he did not want to go back?"

"I'm afraid I'd have to take him, anyway, ma'am. The boy was apprenticed to me. He's not finished his time."

"You have his papers?"

"His what?"

"When there is an apprenticeship, there are forms that have to be filled out."

"I guess I just forgot to bring 'em, ma'am." The man's smile was tolerant but amused. "Next time I'm by this way, I'll show 'em to you. Now I want the boy, and I understand he's here, workin' for you. Name of Wat Tanner."

Mary Breydon walked around behind the table and filled her cup. "I am sure the simplest way to arrange this," she said, "would be for us to meet in Laporte where we can see the judge. We can place the matter before him."

The smile left the man's face. He was growing irritated. "I am afraid I can't wait for that. I've ridden all the way in the rain—"

"Where are you from, Mr.—?"

"Williams," he said. "I'm from north of here, up nigh the Wyoming border. Now if you'll let me have the boy—"

"I am very sorry. You cannot have him. If you wish to meet me in Laporte before the judge, I am sure something can be arranged.

"Although," she added, "I very much doubt the boy wants to go with you."

"Ma'am, I've come a long way. I'm not goin' back without that boy. Now you turn him over to me, or—"

"Or what, Mr. Williams? The boy is here, in my care, and I shall not turn him over to you without an order from a judge."

"What if I just take him?"

"You wouldn't take him very far with a belly full of lead, would you?" The voice was casual, even pleasant.

She did not turn, keeping her eyes on Williams, the cup of hot coffee in her hand.

Temple Boone moved farther into the room from the door of the pantry. His hat was wet, his jacket dripping.

"Howdy, Boone." Williams's tone was as quiet as Boone's. "I didn't expect to see you around here."

"Roundin' up stock for the stage line," Boone explained conversationally. "It's a livin'."

"If you like what you're doin'," Williams suggested, "I'd say stick with it and you'll do a lot more livin'. We want that boy, Boone."

"Seems like a lot of fuss over one youngster," Boone said, "but like the lady said, you can meet in front of a judge an' make your claim." He smiled suddenly, a flashing, handsome smile. "And I'd bet a new saddle it wouldn't be the first judge you've been up before."

Slowly, Williams put down his cup, resting his fingertips on the edge of the table as if about to rise.

"I wouldn't if I was you," Temple said. "You never seen the day."

Slowly, the hands eased back into the center of the table, one of them reaching for the empty cup. "They won't like it," he said hoarsely. "They sent me for the boy."

"Leave him alone," Boone replied. "He's doing no harm to

anybody. You boys push him and he's liable to get scared—or mad. Might make all the difference."

"You tell that to Denver."

Boone sat down opposite Williams. "Denver an' me don't see eye to eye. We never did. You just tell him the boy is doin' all right and to leave him be."

"You wouldn't think a youngster would be that canny," Williams said. "He left just no trail at all. I'd run out of chances until I heard somebody at Virginia Dale Station say there was a boy-kid workin' down here."

Williams drained his cup, seeking for the few last drops. "You can have him. He's a durned thief, anyways. Stole Johnny's boots off him after he was dead."

"I did no such thing!" Wat Tanner spoke from the door. "Johnny asked me to pull 'em off. Promised his ma he'd never die with his boots on. Then he told me they was almost new, and I was to take them.

"I said they was too big, and he said I'd grow into them. He said some of you boys would steal 'em, anyway. He was the one tol' me to git, said your lot was no fit comp'ny for a boy."

Williams flushed, stealing a shamed look at Mary Breydon. "I don't believe he said any such thing! Anyway, who was Johnny to talk?"

"He was best of that crowd," Boone said. "Why else was he killed?"

Williams got up. "I'm ridin'."

"You do that. And you tell Denver Cross the boy is a friend of mine, and so are the folks at this station. You just tell him that and make sure he hears it."

When Williams had gone, Mary Breydon accepted the breakfast Matty fixed for her and sat down across from Boone. "You have some strange friends, Mr. Boone."

Boone smiled. "It's a big country, but there aren't all that many people. Sooner or later, you get to know everybody. Ofttimes the men who are outlaws and those who are the law once worked side by side or fought in the war together.

"Take you, now. You've just met Williams, and he's an outlaw. You've become mighty important to Scant Luther, another man of doubtful character."

He smiled widely. "Seems to me, Mrs. Breydon, that you have some strange friends!"

She laughed. "All right. But thank you for speaking up for Wat."

"He'd do as much for me," Boone said lightly. "After all, he's one of the few of us who is really 'western.' Everybody out here is from somewhere else."

"You, too, Mr. Boone?"

He ignored the question. "Seen you unloadin' some books. Do you read books like that?"

"I do."

"Never read me many books." He paused, embarrassed. "Always figured to, sometime. I seen a few around. One time, a long while back, I worked some in a store back in Missouri. They had all manner of books. Folks goin' West used to buy 'em. I just couldn't believe there was so many folks who not only could read but wanted to."

"If one has a book, Mr. Boone, one is never alone. They will talk to you when you want to listen, and when you tire of what they are saying, you just close the book. It will be waiting for you when you come back to it."

He pushed back from the table. "I'd better get the team ready. The stage will be comin' in."

When he left, trailed by Wat, she looked after him. "He's a strange man, Matty."

"Good-lookin', too," Matty said, her expression innocent. "He's a fine figure of a man."

"I suppose so. My husband was, too, and I miss him, Matty."

"You're a young woman."

Mary flashed her a quick look. "I wasn't thinking of that. Marshall was a wonderful man. I doubt if I should ever be so lucky again."

"The odds would seem to be against it, ma'am, but some women just seem to attract the good man. Others just attract the good-lookin' rascals."

She went to the stove. "I'll just warm up some of that stew. It is a wet, unpleasant morning."

Mary walked to the window and looked down the road. Since arriving, she had been nowhere, done nothing but get

the station and the cottage into some kind of shape and find her
way in a strange situation. When the weather cleared, she
would get a horse and ride down the valley. Or she might even
go into Laporte.

It was an old town, although small. Once it had been
mentioned as a possible state capital, but Denver had grown
rapidly after the gold discoveries. Yet a visit to Laporte was an
essential. There were things she needed and some she could
no longer do without. Also, she needed a hostler here at the
station. Boone was just helping until they got settled.

The rain on the roof was a pleasant sound. Matty opened the
stove and added some fuel. They used the fireplace only occasionally now, although she had always loved an open fire.

Her thoughts returned to the events of the morning. What
did those men want with Wat? Williams, she gathered, was a
man of doubtful character, probably an outlaw. And who *was*
Wat? The man called Johnny, of whom they had spoken, was
obviously not his father, yet what was the connection? She
must ask Boone. He would probably tell her nothing, for these
western men were oddly reticent about talking of each other
unless they had something good to say.

She *was* lonely. Until now, she had been too busy to think of
such things, certainly to think of herself. She was lonely for
someone with whom she could talk, not just of horses, the
station, or of the people here but of books, music, the greater,
wider world. Not necessarily, she realized, a better world.

There was little leisure here, little time for self-examination
or things concerned with the self. People here were, for good
or ill, too busy doing things, living, building, creating in a
physical sense. There was almost no backbiting, little gossip as
such. What talk there was concerned events, people, cattle,
horses, the prospects in any one of a dozen fields. Nobody
seemed to be sitting still; nobody had empty hands. There
were some who might only be stirring up dust, but they were
trying.

She must not allow herself to stagnate. There were books, as
Temple Boone had reminded her, and she should read to Peg,
and to Wat, for that matter. Standing by the window looking

out on the rain-wet morning, she turned over in her mind the men she had met.

One and all, they seemed inwardly strong; each was responsible for himself. If one of them made a wrong step, he seemed willing to accept the blame, and nobody asked favors of another. Deliberately, intentionally, they were self-reliant.

Later, when Boone came in from the stable, she mentioned it to him. "Ma'am? You ever notice a child? If he falls down and hurts himself, most times he won't start to cry until he's close to his mama. There's no sense in crying if there's nobody to listen. Out here, a man does for himself, or it ain't done. You just don't wait for somebody to do it for you. And there's no sense in cryin' or complainin' because nobody has the time to listen.

"If somebody is hurtin', somebody will help and then go on about his business. They'll help you cross a river, pull a wagon out of the mud, splint a broken leg, round up cattle, or whatever. They'll *help* you, ma'am, but unless you're down sick or somethin', they won't do it for you. Everybody saddles his own broncs out here."

"Mr. Boone? It is probably needless to warn you, but be careful. Be very careful. I recognized the man you called Williams. He was one of the guerrillas who raided my home during the war. While the North and the South were fighting, they were riding, looting, burning, and killing."

"Seems likely."

"My husband saw their leader out here. He started to accuse him, and the man shot him. He killed my husband, Mr. Boone. And my husband was a very good shot."

"Bein' a good shot is one thing. Sometimes it simply ain't enough. People who do their shootin' out here don't waste around."

"I know. I am afraid Marshall was not expecting it just that way. He was prepared to fight, but the other man just drew his gun and shot Marshall."

"I suspect. You know who that other man was?"

"His name was Jason Flandrau."

SEVEN

There was a long moment of silence. A stick fell in the stove, and Matty came in from the cottage. She looked across at them, then asked suddenly, "Mum? Is something wrong, then?"

Temple Boone did not respond, but he put his cup down and leaned his forearms on the table. "Ma'am? Have you any idea why Jason Flandrau shot your husband?"

"Perhaps because he expected Marshall to challenge him. Perhaps because he expected to be shot."

"Listen to me now," Boone said, "and listen close. You're a mighty smart woman, and nobody is goin' to have to draw you pictures.

"Jason Flandrau is callin' himself 'Colonel' Jason Flandrau now, and he's bein' spoken of for governor. He's livin' down to Denver, an' livin' mighty high on the hog, if you know what I mean. He's joined the church. He's been singin' in the choir, takin' a big hand in all the public meetin's.

"The minute he seen your husband, he saw an end to all that, for once the story got out, he'd be finished. Folks might accept a former Confederate, although there's considerable doubt of that, but nobody has any use for a guerrilla. They'd run him out of the country, maybe hang him. He claimed self-defense, ma'am, and he was surely tellin' the truth. He had to kill your husband before he could talk, and he done it."

"I suppose you are right."

"Doesn't that mean something else to you, ma'am?"

"Of course, Mr. Boone. I see that he must kill me, too, as soon as he discovers I am here."

"You ever met him?"

"No, I have not."

"No matter. Soon as he hears about you, he will know what he has to do, and he will hear. There's already been a lot of talk up an' down the line about you."

"About me?"

"Ma'am, you're a mighty beautiful woman, and beautiful women are scarce in this country right now. Sooner or later, he's goin' to hear about you and make the connection. As far as that goes, Williams will probably rush to tell him. He recognized you, didn't he?"

"I doubt it. I do not believe he ever saw me before. I saw him from our window. I was inside the house until it started to burn; then we fled out the back. No, I don't believe he ever saw me."

She paused. "Mr. Boone? Why did they want Wat?"

"Surprised you haven't guessed. They want him because he knows where they are hid out. Don't you see? They've found a place, and that was where Wat ran away from. They're afraid he'll tell the law, or somebody. If they get him, they'll either keep him locked up, or they'll kill him."

"Kill a little boy?"

"Ma'am, in Lawrenceville and some other places, they killed women, children, and old men. Besides, the stakes are bigger now. Jason Flandrau has not only been mentioned for governor, he wants to *be* governor. You've got to get out of here, Mrs. Breydon. You've got to take that little girl of yours and run."

"I can't." She looked directly into his eyes. "This is my home now. This is my job. As far as Jason Flandrau is concerned, he will not be governor if I can help it."

"He'll know that, ma'am. He will also know that with you

operating this stage station, you've no place to hide. Any passersby, any passenger on the stage, anybody who wants to lay up in the woods back yonder, any one of them can kill you."

"This is my job. I shall stay here."

Boone stared at her, then got up quickly. "All right, but you be careful, d'you hear?"

"He was one of those who came down from the hills and burned my home. He ran off our cattle. He killed a couple of our people who got in his way. And then he killed my husband. Oh, I'll be careful, Mr. Boone, but I shall go down to Denver and tell them."

"He'd laugh at you. So would other folks. Ma'am, didn't you *hear* me? He's a church member over yonder. He sings in the choir, gives money to good causes. He's a pillar of the community, and who are you? You're just some no-account woman who runs a stage station. Least, that's what they'll say."

Of course, he was right. Long after he was gone, she sat in her chair thinking. Matty came up to her and stood across the table. "Mum? I heard what was said. I wasn't eavesdroppin' or the like. You've got to be careful, mum."

"Yes," she agreed, "I must be careful. I have Peg to think of, and Wat." She looked up at Matty with a wan smile. "See? I am already thinking of him as one of the family."

"He's a good lad. I doubt you've noticed, mum, but he's tryin' to improve his table manners. I see him watching you and Peg. He makes his bed ever' morning, too."

Mary Breydon heard, but she did not reply. Jason Flandrau was evil. He was cruel, vicious, and a thief. To think of him being governor or holding any public office was to shudder. Somehow, someway, she must defeat him. But Boone was right. To many of the women around Denver and Laporte, she would be suspect. She was working at a job usually only held by a man—something not quite "nice."

The stage came in, and she glanced at the passengers as they stepped down, suddenly aware that she must pay careful attention not only to who they were but to their actions.

Two of the eight passengers were men obviously bound for the gold camps to the west, one a drummer peddling, as he soon let them know, hand-me-downs for men who bought their suits off the shelf. There was a rather pretty young woman who was, she said, a performer. There was an older woman on her way to Fort Laramie, traveling with her husband, a captain in the army, stationed there.

The seventh was a tall, very thin man with a neatly trimmed handle-bar mustache and auburn hair. He had the air of a gentleman, but his clothes, although still neat after the long stage trip, were shabby.

He glanced very quickly at Mary, frowned slightly, and looked away, then back again, as if puzzled.

Wilbur came inside behind her and said, "One man got off right up the line. Preston Collier had a carriage waitin' for him. Englishman, by the sound of him, and some high muckety-muck by the look."

"Collier? He's the rancher, isn't he?"

"He is that, rich as all get out," Wilbur replied as Boone joined them. "Has him a ranch home with white pillars and two good-lookin' daughters so prim sugar wouldn't melt in their mouths. His wife's the same type. This here Englishman brought some guns along. Says he's goin' to hunt bears and buffalo and such. He'll be lucky if he doesn't get himself killed."

She laughed, then said, "Don't jump to conclusions, Wilbur. Some of those Englishmen can really shoot. When I was a girl, some of them used to stop at our house while hunting in the Bull Run Mountains or the Blue Ridge."

"Yes, ma'am, you could be right. There was an Irishman or Englishman named Gore. He come out a few years back and shot everything in sight. He shot up enough wild critturs to fatten a tribe of Shoshones, left most of it lay. Me, I never shot anything least I wanted to eat it." Wilbur walked out to check on the horses.

"Collier's all right," Boone said. "He's a solid man. A good cattleman. I don't always hold with his politics, but his word is as good as his bond." Boone hesitated, then commented casual-ly, "If a man wanted to run for office in this part of the territory, Preston Collier would be a man to cultivate."

Mary glanced at Boone, but he was looking away, watching

the passengers filing in to the table. Was he trying to tell her something? To warn her?

Temple Boone was a puzzle. Just who *was* he? Where did he come from? There was much about him that puzzled her, yet he said nothing of his background, and the little she had heard was that he had worked at a usual round of frontier jobs. Wat . . . she must ask Wat. He seemed to know a good bit about everyone.

For that matter, who was Wat? Had he no family? Where was his mother? A "sagebrush orphan," they called him, a name given to children whose parents had died or disappeared. Usually, they attached themselves to some other family or found work helping on a ranch until they finally drifted on to wherever such people go.

Well, that would not happen to Wat! He was a nice boy, and she would see he had a chance. Peg liked him, and they were close enough in age that they could be companions.

Nobody asked questions out here. That was one of the first things she had to learn. Every man was taken at face value until he proved himself otherwise. What you had been before was unimportant.

The West, she had come to understand, was a place where you started over. When you came West, you wiped off the slate, and whatever you were to be began here and now. If you had courage, did your job, and were a man of your word, nobody cared whatever you might have been. It was a good thing, she decided. There should always be a place for people to begin again.

Some, like herself, had lost loved ones. Some had gone bankrupt, some had gotten themselves into trouble with the law, into debts that were a burden, some were simply men and women who did not fit into any pattern. They were not the kind to become tellers in the corner bank, grocery clerks, ministers, or lawyers. They were born with a restlessness in them, an urge to move, to get on with it. If you proved yourself a responsible person, nobody cared where you came from.

She was learning, she realized, and ridding herself of preconceived ideas. She had heard the West was lawless, but that had been a mistake. Organized law was, for the most part, remote and far away. However, there were unwritten laws that all obeyed, and if there were a few who did not, the response was apt to be abrupt and very, very final.

The West was tolerant, to a point. When tolerance reached its limit, there was usually a rope or a bullet waiting.

The passengers ate, got up, stretched, and walked outside, lingering around, waiting until the last minute to board the stage.

Wilbur came to the door, his whip in one hand, a cup of coffee in the other. He stopped beside Mary.

"Wilbur? Do you know Jason Flandrau?"

"I do, ma'am."

"If you see him down this way, tell me, will you?"

"Yes, ma'am." He handed her his empty cup. "He'll be comin' down soon, ma'am. He'll be wantin' to talk to Preston Collier."

She was not afraid now, yet she knew what fear was, and the only time she had ever been frightened was when Jason Flandrau and his guerrillas had raided their plantation, striking suddenly across the mountains from their hideout in Kentucky.

She fled with Peg in her arms and a neighbor girl, guided by Beloit, an old black man whom her husband had bought and freed several years before. He hid them in a cave behind some bushes, and they had seen their homes go up in flames, seen the stock driven off, and Beloit, who had run back to get some papers from the house, shot down in cold blood by Flandrau himself.

Now he was here. He had destroyed her home, killed her husband, and to survive and become what he intended, he must kill her.

What she had sought here was a new start, to build a new home, to make a living for herself and her daughter, but Flandrau was here, too, and she had no choice. Should she sit by weakly and be destroyed?

Long ago, a soldier visiting her father had said something she remembered. "The secret of victory is to attack, always attack. If you have ten thousand men, attack. If you have but two men, attack. There is always a way."

Was there? What could she do? Yet the idea was right. She must not sit by, waiting to be killed, waiting to be destroyed. She must move herself.

But what could she, a woman, do? What weapons did she have?

She had the truth, yet she was not so naive as to believe the truth alone would prevail.

The truth was a weapon, and if wisely used, it might destroy him. She did not intend to sit by and wait for attack. She would choose her time, and then she would move. But what time? When? How?

She must have a pistol. Tomorrow. Tomorrow, she would go into Laporte and buy one.

She watched the dust settle after the departure of the stage; then she walked out to the stable. Wat was there, pitchfork in hand. He was, she noted, keeping things neat and clean. "Thank you, Wat. Everything looks very nice."

"It's a job, ma'am."

"Wat? You seem to know most of the people around here. How do you happen to know so many?"

"I sort of watch and listen."

"Where are your family, Wat?"

"I got no family." He looked up at her, then quickly away. "I got nobody."

"Now that isn't a nice thing to say. What about me? What about Peg?"

"You ain't kinfolk."

"There is more than one kind of kinfolk, Wat. Some are kin by blood and some by heart. Peg wants to think you are her brother, and I like that. You have a family, Wat, if you want it."

"Yes, ma'am."

"What happened to your family, Wat? Your father and mother?"

He shuffled his feet, then stabbed at the earthen floor with his pitchfork. "Mama died when I was two, maybe three. I remember her a little. Pa, he was shot."

"Shot? By whom?"

"It makes no dif'rence."

They were interrupted by the sound of hoofs. "Riders comin'," Wat said. "Two of them."

She glanced out of the stable door. Two men on horseback, and they were strangers.

EIGHT

Long ago, her father had told her to *see*. "Not many do,
Mary. Learn to see what you are looking at." And about
these riders there was something different.

"They have fine horses," she said aloud.

"Yes, ma'am," Wat said. "No cowhand can afford horses like
that. They are either mighty well off, or they are outlaws."

"Outlaws?"

"Yes, ma'am, an outlaw needs a horse that can run. A horse
with stayin' quality, too. He dasn't trust himself to just any ol'
crow bait."

"Wat, please go into the station and tell Matty not to mention me. Just feed them and let them ride on. I'll wait until
they are inside, and then I'll go over to the house."

"You scared of them?"

"Not scared, just careful." She put her hand on his shoulder.
"Wat, I am going to tell you something, but keep it to yourself.
My husband was shot and killed by a man named Jason Flandrau.
He shot my husband because of what we knew about him, and
he does not want people out here to know.

"He killed my husband to keep him from talking, and he may have heard that I am here."

Wat walked across to the station as the men were tying their horses. She saw the door open and close. The men looked around, then followed him in, and as soon as the door closed, when they would be looking about the room, she crossed to the house.

Peg looked up from the tablet where she was drawing. "Mama? What's the matter?"

"There are some men at the station. I do not want them to see me."

"Did they?"

"I don't believe so. We will have to wait and see."

Inside the station, Wat moved over beside Matty. "How's about some of that pie? As long as there's only the two of us to eat it—"

"You'll have to wait until I feed these gentlemen. They might want some pie." Her attention caught at his comment "only the two of us." He was staring at her, his eyes intent as if trying to tell her something.

"I know you got to feed these fellers, but if there's any left . . . I mean, you don't eat pie, and that leaves only me."

Matty glanced toward the two men, two strong, rough-looking men, both wearing guns. Of course, nearly everybody out here did wear guns, but—

"Coffee?" she asked. "Is it coffee you're wanting?"

"And a bite to eat if you've something put by."

"We've a bit of stew left, and we've bread, fresh baked by meself."

"We'll have it." The younger man glanced around. "We heard there was a woman runnin' the station, but I'd no thought she'd be Irish."

"Are you Irish yourself, then? You've a bit of the look."

"Aye, a bit. My grandmother was from Donegal." He glanced around again. "Is it you who runs the station?"

"Who else? Could the boy run it, now? He's long in the country, though, and I couldna do it without him."

She put down two cups and filled them. "But I didna come for that, not for runnin' of a station or what all. I come for the gold they said was lyin' about everywhere."

Taking a long-handled wooden spoon, she began dishing up stew. " 'Twas my wish to go back to Ireland a rich girl and have the pick o' the lads there."

"You're dreamin', girl." The older man spoke harshly. "How much gold have you seen? It's here, but there's only a few of them has it."

"You watch. I shall find my gold and go home a great lady."

The younger one asked, "Did you come right here from the old country? Or did you stop in Virginia?"

"Virginia? I dinna ken the place. 'Twas to Boston I came and worked there until I could get the fare for the stage to come west. It was California where I was bound, but when I heard there was gold in Colorado and it was a thousand mile the closer, I chose Colorado."

There was no more talk. They settled to their eating, and as Matty had noticed, eating in the West was a serious business not to be interrupted by idle conversation. From time to time, she refilled their cups. She knew tough men when she saw them, and these were all of that.

Where was Mary Breydon? It was unlike her to leave Matty to handle things alone. She glanced at Wat, and he stretched, brushing a finger past his lips as he did so.

Trouble, was it? She refilled the teakettle and stirred the fire. The water in the kettle had been hot, and soon there would be more.

"Meetin' the stage?" she asked.

"Passin' through. Headin' west."

One of them muttered something to the other, and the older man said, "Ain't likely."

" . . . what I think," the younger man said. "Some mistake."

They finished eating, and one of the men rolled a smoke. The younger glanced around again. "Tidy," he said, "right tidy."

"Thank you, sir! It's the only way a poor girl can hold a job these days, to do something better than the men."

The younger man got up. "Come on, Joe. We'll see the boss in Laporte."

They went out the door, stepped into their saddles, and rode away.

Wat turned to Matty. "I thought I knew him! That's Turkey Joe Longman. He's a horse thief and gunman, only he's never been caught at it. I don't know the younger one."

When the sound of hoofs had died away, Mary came back to the station. Matty turned as she came in. "Wat says he knows the older one. He's a horse thief."

"So is the younger one." Mary Breydon's eyes showed her anger. "The horse he's riding was one of ours from back home. I know that horse, and he would know me, I think."

"It's been how long, ma'am?"

"Almost two years since that horse was stolen. He was one of the last ones driven off by Flandrau's men."

"Can you say for sure it was him?"

"I can say it, but I cannot prove it, and he was using another name then. Flandrau was the name he used when he was not robbing and stealing."

"We must tell Mr. Boone, ma'am. He will know what to do."

"What to do is my problem, not his. I'll not be getting him into a shooting because of my troubles. This is for me to do."

"You've made friends, ma'am, good friends. They'll not see you put upon."

"Leave them out of it. I'll handle it."

But how? She could not continue to hide whenever a stranger came by. She had done so this once because she needed time. There was a chance now they would not realize for a few days, at least, that Matty was not the woman in charge. Then they would come back.

"They'll not be fooled," Wat said. "By now there will be talk of you all along the line. Ma'am, I know cowboys, and I know the West, and by now they will be speakin' of you from El Paso to Uvalde to Salt Lake. A good-lookin' woman who can *cook*?

"Word gets around, ma'am. The West has no secrets. There's little enough that's news, and a man in El Paso will know what the town marshal looks like in Denver, he will know there's a card sharp in Kansas City who looks at his watch just before he deals. They know there's something crooked going on, but nobody's caught him at it yet. So they will know you're here."

"Thank you, Wat. I needed a little time, just a little."

"Beggin' your pardon, ma'am, but you're goin' to need a lot more than that. Those are mean men, mighty mean."

She stood looking out the window, looking down the road. Of course, Wat was right. All she had done was to gain a little time, time to think, to plan.

Of course, Jason Flandrau must be careful. To go further with his plans, he must not allow any taint of suspicion to touch him. He must seem to have nothing at all to do with what happened, so it was unlikely he would use any men who were known to work for him or be friendly to him.

Whatever else he might be, Jason Flandrau was no fool. He had acted quickly to kill her husband, but he had no choice, and that was a gun battle, and there were many men in Colorado and the West who had engaged in gun battles. Why even Andrew Jackson had once killed a man in a gunfight!

To kill a woman was another thing, so it would be done with care by somebody unconnected to him, by somebody . . . perhaps even a renegade Indian?

She must get a pistol.

She would go into Laporte, for, of course, they needed much else. There were odds and ends of clothing she must obtain for Peg and herself and a little other shopping. And she must be thinking of schooling for Peg, and as there were no schools close by, she must handle that herself. For Peg and Wat, she reminded herself.

Long ago, her father had taught her to shoot, and she remembered what he had said. "A gun is a responsibility. Never shoot blind. Always know what you are shooting at and never shoot unless there is no other alternative. And consider every gun as loaded. Most of them are."

She must think. The first item was clear and obvious. She might never tell anyone about Flandrau's guerrilla activities, but he could not be sure of that. He had killed her husband; now he would kill her. So she must consider how it might be done and who might do it. Coolly, cold-bloodedly, she must consider every aspect and then be prepared.

She was not a man who might be challenged and killed, as her husband had been. They might hold up the stage and kill her in the process, but already she had learned enough of western ways to know that even the worst of men would hesitate at killing a woman. Kill a man and the West might shrug, but kill a woman and men would arise in their wrath and hunt down the killer and hang him without hesitation.

Ambush . . . shot while crossing the area from the stage station to her dwelling or moving about between the barn and the corral.

Somebody hidden up in the trees on the low hillside with a horse waiting back in the brush. There could be other ways, but that was the most obvious and the one she must consider.

Her father, an old army man, had once said that a battle well planned was half won. Perhaps. There was always the unexpected, but if one had prepared for every contingency, one could then cope with the unexpected. She must be cool; she must be objective.

Nothing in her life had prepared her for this, yet when she came to think of it, she had often heard her husband and father talking of war, Indian fights on the frontier, and there were some things she remembered. She could not, would not, ask for help. That was not the way it was done on the frontier, but even if it had been, what right had she to embroil others in her problems, perhaps at the risk of their lives?

Attack, her father had said, always attack.

To protect herself was not enough; she must not permit a man of Jason Flandrau's type to come to a position of authority.

Who was it who told her that her neighbor, whom she had never met, was a political power as well as a wealthy rancher? What was his name? Collier, Preston Collier. She must meet him, and soon.

Who would oppose Flandrau in running for office? Who stood to lose most if he won? Whoever he was, he was a potential ally, and she would need all the help she could get. Yet she could not come right out and accuse Flandrau, for how could she prove it? This was far from Virginia, Kentucky, and Ohio where he had operated before going West to Missouri and Kansas. Those who might have known of his activities as a guerrilla were scattered, still in the armed forces or perhaps even killed. It would be her unsupported word against his, and he had been making himself prominent in church circles in Denver and elsewhere, had avoided the saloons and gambling halls, and had already won some standing in the area. As for her, she was just a stranger, a woman who, of all things, operated a stage station.

She turned away from the window and glanced at Wat, eating a piece of apple pie. Wat, that strange, wild boy from only God knew where.

"Wat," she said suddenly, "if I had a son, I would want him to be like you."

Startled, Wat looked up, his face flushing with embarrassment. She crossed to him. "I mean it, Wat. I mean every word."

He looked down quickly, tears in his eyes. When he looked up, he had blinked them away.

"Ma'am? If you're goin' into Laporte, I think you should leave me go with you. I could circulate around a little."

"We'll see, Wat. I'll go in tomorrow, I think."

"You goin' on the stage? You take the stage, ma'am. It's safer. Wilbur will be drivin', and he's a good whip."

What would she wear? Her traveling suit? She could press that, and the white blouse? Crossing the room, she looked critically at her hair. She'd have to do something with it and make a list of things to do, things to get.

At the head of the list, a pistol.

NINE

Laporte lay quiet in the morning sun. At the hitching rail in front of a saloon were two horses, at the hardware store, a wagon and team.

Wilbur, glancing along the street, helped her from the stage. "Now you be careful, ma'am." He paused. "You going to eat in town? If you are, try the boardin' house yonder. They've got a private room for such as you an' Peg. Might be better. Sometimes those boys forget theirselves and talk rough. They'd be ashamed, ma'am."

"Are you protecting them or me?" She smiled.

"Both." He held out a hand. "You want me to take that list in to Stacy?"

"No, I'll see him myself. There may be some items that call for explanation. In fact, I'll just go in now."

With Peg by the hand, she pushed open the office door and stepped inside.

Mark Stacy was seated in a swivel chair at a roll-top desk. Seeing her, he got quickly to his feet and reached for his coat.

"You needn't, Mr. Stacy. I am not a guest, only an employee!"

He bowed. "Ma'am, here you are always a guest! Out at the station, I'm the guest"—he grinned—"and you *are* an employee!"

"This is the list—"

"Won't you sit down? Please?"

"Well—only for a minute. We have some shopping to do, and I want to get back to the station."

When she was seated, he shuffled some papers on his desk. "Never heard so many nice things said about the grub—the food, I mean. You're making a name for yourself, ma'am."

"I hope Mr. Holladay will approve."

"Let me tell you something, Mrs. Breydon. Ben Holladay doesn't care whether you are man, woman, red, black, or yellow as long as the stages run on time and folks don't complain. But you can bet on one thing. He'll come along one of these days when you least expect it."

He glanced at her. "Ma'am? What happened? With your husband, I mean."

She hesitated, then said quietly, "Major Breydon was wearing a gun in a button-down holster. He was not a gunfighter. He was not used to western ways. He met a man on the street in Julesburg who had reason not to like him. That man simply drew his gun and fired. My husband was killed instantly."

"You know who killed him?"

"It was Jason Flandrau."

"*Jason Flandrau!* Ma'am, you must be mistaken. Mr. Flandrau is not a gunfighter. He's a very respectable and respected gentleman!"

He frowned. "Come to think of it, I recall some talk of Major Breydon being killed, but his killer wasn't named. Fact is, I doubt if anybody knew who he was."

"I knew, Mr. Stacy."

"Was it some old quarrel? Something that happened back East?"

"It was no quarrel. My husband only quarreled with gentlemen, Mr. Stacy, when he quarreled at all, which was rare, indeed. Mr. Flandrau killed my husband because the major recognized him."

Stacy hesitated. There was something here he did not understand. Jason Flandrau was a very popular man in Denver.

Friendly, easygoing, and a free spender who associated only with the most respectable people. Killed because the major *recognized* him?

"I am afraid I don't follow you, Mrs. Breydon."

She arose. "There is no reason why you should. My troubles are my own. One thing I might ask. Do not mention me to Mr. Flandrau and, please, do not repeat this conversation."

"I certainly will not mention it, but I must warn you, ma'am. Mr. Flandrau has many friends. He is a great favorite. More than that—"

"Yes?"

"He has an office right down the street. Over the bank. I believe he is there now."

Taking Peg by the hand, she went out. For a moment, she hesitated. If there had been a way, she would have turned right around and gone back to Cherokee, but there was no way. Not until late in the afternoon. There was nothing to do but do what she came for.

Swiftly, she crossed the street and entered the hardware store. When a man with sleeve protectors came up to her, she said, "I want to buy a pistol."

He glanced at her. The request was not unusual. "I have a fine little twenty-two here, ma'am."

"I do not want a twenty-two. I want a navy pistol, thirty-six caliber."

"That's large for a woman—"

"I have fired them. My husband taught me."

"Oh? That's different, ma'am." He took a pistol from under the counter. "Brand, spankin' new, ma'am. One of the best."

She glanced at it. "I'll take it. I want some powder and ball, too." She had started to turn away to where Peg was looking at some ribbons when she saw the matched derringers. "What are they worth?"

"Ma'am, they are very fine weapons. Small but very well made. Cost you forty dollars for the pair. And they are forty-four caliber, ma'am."

Forty dollars? And she was already buying one pistol. Yet how much was a life worth? "I'll take them. Will you charge them, please?"

"You want to carry them loaded, ma'am? I think—"

"I am leaving on the stage this afternoon, sir. They wouldn't be much good to me unloaded, would they?" She smiled.

He smiled back. "I guess not. I'll load 'em, ma'am." He nodded toward the other side of the store where the dry goods lay. "Looks to me like your sister has found somethin' she likes."

She smiled again. "Thank you, sir. The young lady is my daughter."

"Daughter? Say, you wouldn't be Mrs. Breydon, would you? The one who operates Cherokee? They do say you've the finest grub this side of Georgetown."

"Thank you. I am Mrs. Breydon."

She crossed to the other side of the store. In a few minutes, her other shopping completed, she returned for the loaded guns and left the store.

In the office over the bank, Jason Flandrau stood at the window. He was talking to two men in business suits who were seated near his desk. He turned to face them, his back to the window.

"Gentlemen, you do me honor! To tell you the truth, I have thought of running for governor. I know a bill was introduced with the idea that Colorado would become a state. In such case, I am sure they would prefer the territorial governor they have now to any newcomer. However"—he smiled graciously—"if enough people were to ask me—"

"I am sure they will, Mr. Flandrau. Some of us want a change. We feel a change is essential, and such an up-and-coming man as yourself—Well, we are sure you are what the voters want, Mr. Flandrau."

"You gentlemen understand these things better than I. But if the bill passes, then think of me, and if you wish it, I will run."

He turned back to the window, scarcely able to conceal his elation. Of course, they could not know how he had carefully set the stage for just this to happen, and now—

He looked down into the street. A woman and a small girl were crossing the street, an uncommonly beautiful woman—

He stiffened, and his hands gripped the curtain pole that crossed the middle of the window so hard it nearly snapped.

Mary Breydon! Mary Breydon here! Of all the damned miserable luck! He stared, started to turn away, then looked again, but she was out of sight on the walk below him.

"Is something wrong, Mr. Flandrau?"

He managed a smile. "No, no, of course not. I was just thinking. We could do a lot together, gentlemen. Now if you'll permit me?"

They got to their feet. "Of course. We are interrupting."

"No, but I do have some business. Let us wait, gentlemen, and see what happens to that statehood bill."

When they were gone, Flandrau sat down at his desk. Who would ever have believed Mary Breydon would come West? Had she accompanied her husband, or had she come later because of his death?

He had heard the rumors, of course, but he could not believe that the Mary Breydon he knew would be the woman operating a stage station, yet they had to be one and the same. Turkey Joe had been mistaken then, or he had missed seeing Mary Breydon.

He swore softly but bitterly. Killing Breydon had been one thing; gun duels were happening all the time. In this western country, if you killed an armed enemy, it was to your credit, but another killing of anyone would begin to raise doubts, and the killing of a woman was not to be considered. Yet die she must. She knew too much, and she had too many well-connected friends.

Major Breydon had been a well-liked man. Suppose she got an investigation started? Breydon would have had friends at Fort Collins nearby, and they would certainly investigate if there seemed to be doubtful circumstances. So far, there had been no investigation, as it had appeared to be a cut-and-dried gunfight.

But how? How?

How to be rid of her without any suspicion being directed toward himself?

A simple holdup in which she was killed by accident? No

. . . if a woman was killed, they'd pursue the killers until they were caught, and before being hung, one of them might talk.

A shot from ambush? He would have the area scouted to see if there was a chance that would also permit an escape. Steal an Indian pony and let the killer ride it until he reached a safe spot to switch to another and better horse, probably in the vicinity of an Indian village or camp?

Or an Indian attack on the station? Or men dressed as Indians?

He got up from his desk and walked to the window. There was no sign of her on the street, yet he must not risk being seen by her, and damn it! He wanted a drink!

How long would she be in town? He tried to remember when the next stage left for Cherokee.

Stampede the stage? Set fire to the stage station?

Laporte was virtually a one-street town; at least all the shops and stores as well as the saloons were on the one street, so there was small chance of avoiding anyone you did not wish to see.

If ambush was the way, who could he trust to handle it? Of the old outfit, which had numbered more than sixty men, he had kept but a dozen to bring West with him. The others were scattered, some of them gone to their homes, some slain in the fighting of '63. One by one he considered each man. The killer would have to believe himself in danger, too. Slowly, he began to concoct the story he would tell the man he sent, that if she recognized one of them, she would go at once to the law or to Fort Collins and the army.

Once the job was done, he would eliminate the man who did it. If he was to be governor or senator, he must have a clean slate. He would grow a beard, slowly change his style of dress to a more sober, dignified habit.

As for Mary Breydon—

He would go to Denver and remain there until the job was done. Small chance of her coming on there, and he certainly would avoid Cherokee.

He scowled. Damn it, what about Preston Collier? The rancher was throwing some kind of a party for some English nobleman who was coming to the mountains to hunt, and Collier had invited him.

It was the best chance he had to cultivate Collier, who was something of a power in a political sense, always behind the scenes but always in on the action. That was what they said of Collier. Besides, there would be others present, and it would be a good chance to enter that more rarefied social strata where he was still unknown. Yet it was small risk. Collier might think of inviting a woman who ran a stage station, but his wife certainly would not, nor her daughters.

Mary Breydon gathered the last of her packages, her eyes straying toward the small shelf of books on sale. They were, as always, the classics, most of which she had read, but what of Peg? And Wat?

"You're interested in books, ma'am?"

She looked around at the storekeeper, surprised. "I've only a few, but folks like the very best. They like books they can read over and over. Right down the street, there's a bookstore. He carries quite a stock, along with pencils, paper, notions, and such. That's where Mark Stacy buys his books."

"Mark Stacy? Somehow I did not imagine him to be a reader."

"Some of these folks surprise you, ma'am. You never know who is the reader or who has the education. That's why there's few western towns without a bookstore."

The storekeeper paused, then said, "He's a mighty fine man, Mr. Stacy is. Single, too. Was I a widow-lady—"

She turned around and looked at him coolly. "Sir, this 'widow-lady' is quite content. I have my daughter, and I have my work to do. Also, my marriage was a very happy one."

"I just thought—"

"No doubt you did, sir, but my personal affairs are just that, my personal affairs. Thank you, sir."

She was angry, and it showed. Out on the street, she stopped, fuming. "That man—!"

"I thought he was a nice man."

"He's a busybody. My life is no business of his. Let's go home!"

"We aren't going to the bookstore?"

"Another time, Peg. Another time."

Yet she glanced down the street toward the beckoning sign, a narrow, two-story building huddled between a harness shop and a bakery.

TEN

Not until she was seated in the darkness of the stage with Peg asleep against her shoulder did she admit she was frightened. Alone in the darkness, she fought back the tears. If anything happened to her, what would become of Peg?

Jason Flandrau was in Laporte. He had many friends there and was a respected man. He had both money and power. He was a careful man who knew how to cultivate the most influential people. If she told what she knew of him, who would listen? He need only to smile tolerantly and make some mild comment about hysterical women.

She was nobody here. Back home she could have gone to a senator, a member of the cabinet, even to the president himself. Now she was just a woman who operated a stage station.

All that she had been was far away in Washington or Richmond where they were busy fighting a war. If she were killed out here, it would be weeks, perhaps months, before anybody back there even heard of it.

Her father, a prominent man with political leverage, was

dead. Her husband was dead. She was alone, with no one to turn to.

Of course, she had friends in Virginia and Maryland, many of them, but they were far from here. By the time they realized her situation, it would be too late. Moreover, they and their families were involved in a war, and she had no right to distract them with her troubles. Nor was it in her to call for help. "The strongest," her father often said, "is he who stands alone."

She was not weak. She could not be, dared not be. This was her battle, and she must fight it, win it alone.

Yet if something happened to her, what would become of Peg?

She must think of that coolly, realistically. It was all right to be brave, but what if her bravery destroyed her daughter? She was not one of those fools who believe they are invulnerable, that nothing could ever happen to her. Death had no respect for individuals. It came to the good, the bad, and the indifferent with equal indifference.

She must consider all aspects, for the man who was her enemy was utterly ruthless, would kill her without a qualm . . . or have her killed.

She was still thinking of that when the stage rolled into Cherokee Station and the door opened, light streaming from the stage-station door across the legs of the horses, the wheels, and the step she took down into the dust.

Wilbur offered her a hand down, then lifted Peg from the stage. Peg awakened, clinging to her hand. "Mama? Are we home?" she asked sleepily.

Mary Breydon looked at the shabby station. "Yes, honey, we're home."

"The little one is all in, ma'am," Wilbur said. He removed his hat and wiped his brow with a sleeve. "Ma'am? If there's anything I can do? Are you in trouble, ma'am?"

She looked at him with a wan smile. "Yes, Wilbur, I am in trouble, but it is my trouble. There's nothing, nothing anyone can do."

Gathering her skirt, holding Peg with the other hand, she

took a step up to the stoop, then hesitated. "There is one thing, Wilbur. If you see any strange riders—you know the kind—will you tell me?"

When she had gone inside, Temple Boone came from the shadows near the corral. "What's wrong, Wilbur?"

"Damned if I know, but something is. She wouldn't admit to it, but she's a scared woman." He paused. "Boone? What d'you know about Jason Flandrau?"

Boone turned his eyes to Wilbur. "He's been around. Right now he's bein' so sanctimonious butter wouldn't melt in his mouth, but he's got a way about him. The way he takes in a street, the way he walks, where he sits . . . somewhere he's given himself reason to be careful. Others may not see it, but anybody who's been on the dodge knows the signs."

"Stacy asked me what I knew about him. She says Flandrau killed her husband over to Julesburg at the time of the Cheyenne trouble."

"I heard the talk. This officer—her husband—called him by name, and Flandrau shot him, quick as that." Boone took a cigar from his pocket. "Flandrau said the officer had threatened to shoot him on sight, but the way I heard it, that officer never even had his holster unbuttoned. He never had a chance."

Wilbur shrugged. "You make war talk, you'd better be ready to make war," he said. "You know as well as me that if you threaten to kill a man, he can shoot you wherever he finds you. It's simple common sense. What do we know about Flandrau?"

Boone lit his cigar. "What do we know about anybody? Folks don't ask questions out here. It's what you do, not who you were, that matters. The way I hear it, he's a churchgoing man, doesn't waste around with anybody but those who carry weight, who have the power. Only for a churchgoing man he was awful fast with that gun. Folks said he shot only once, but there were two bullet holes not an inch apart."

"That fast, was he?"

"Fast and accurate, and you don't get that good unless there's a trail behind you somewhere."

Temple Boone went into the barn. He glanced toward the tack room where Wat slept. Softly, he said, "Are you awake?"

"Yes, sir."

" 'Sir,' is it now?"

"Yes, sir. She'd like me to speak respectful."

"Wat. She's a good woman, and she's in trouble."

"Yes, sir." After a moment's hesitation, he said, "A couple of men rode by t' other day. Nosin' around. One of them was Turkey Joe Longman."

"Know him, do you?"

"I know him. The other one is new. Younger, part Irish. Wears his gun on the left side, butt forward."

"Notice his gun?"

"One o' them Dance pistols made by the South durin' the war. Looks like a Colt."

"They were copies, but different. You've got sharp eyes, youngster."

"He's slick with it, too. That's what I think. Turkey Joe kind of steps aside for him."

"They didn't see Mrs. Breydon?"

"No, sir. She kep' from sight. They talked to Matty, and when they left, they talked like there'd been some mistake." After a moment, Wat said, "They asked Matty if she come West by way of Virginia."

"Thanks, Wat. You go to sleep now."

He was spreading his blanket in the hay when Wat said, "Mr. Boone? We got to watch out for her. She's new in this country."

"We will, Wat. We will."

Brushing her hair before the mirror, Mary thought back over the day's activities. Mark Stacy, she decided, was a nice man and without doubt a good man at his job.

Deliberately, she avoided thoughts of Flandrau and her own problems. There would be time enough for that. Now she must think of her job. Mark Stacy might be pleasant, but he was also a division agent, or whatever they called them, and with him the division would come first, and that meant every station on the route. The Cherokee Trail, she had heard on the way out, was the toughest division on the Overland Trail. He was obviously skeptical about her ability to handle it. Not just her ability but that of any woman in what had always been considered a man's job, so she would try a little harder.

Food along the line, as she had discovered while traveling it, was far from the best, so that was one mark in her favor. She decided then they would make doughnuts, and she'd make some cookies. It wasn't much but would probably send the passengers on their way, pleased with what they had found.

Later, she would have a patch plowed or dug up, and she would plant a kitchen garden. It would help a little and would vary the fare.

Cleanliness first, good food second, and always fast and efficient service and correct timing. Coming West, she had discovered that if one did not rush through a meal, one left much of it behind. Hence, the food must be ready to serve the instant they walked through the door, and she would delay the teams just a little to provide for the time to eat. Take the first team to the barn before the second was brought out. It was not the policy, but it would provide just the margin of difference. She would time the meals, time the changing of the teams. It could be worked out, she was sure.

Peg . . . she must think of her education, and there was no school close by. Marshall had read to Peg, and she loved it, so she would do the same. They had a few books, and when those were finished, there was the bookstore in town.

She asked Temple Boone about it at breakfast. "Does well, ma'am, mighty well. Folks out here are hungry for something to read. I've seen 'em memorize the labels on tin cans just for something to read.

"Never read much, myself. Seen a few plays from time to time. That *Hamlet* now, seen that one twice. There was some mighty fine talkin' in that play, but folks were makin' a lot of what they called his indecision, and that seemed kind of silly to me. After all, he had no evidence of wrongdoin' there, only the word of a ghost.

"Now a man's got to be reasonable. A man who would attack somebody or even accuse somebody on the word of a ghost would have to be off his trail mentally.

"A couple of years ago, back in St. Louis, a man killed another man with an ax 'because the Lord told him to,' and they ruled him insane. It's the same thing. Hamlet wasn't indecisive; he just didn't have enough evidence for a sane man, so he tried to lead them to betray themselves."

He sipped his coffee. "My mother was Danish, and she used to tell me stories, and one of them was a story about Hamlet. That's an old, old story in Iceland, and there are many versions of it."

"I would not have guessed you were Danish."

"I'm not. Actually, although my mother was raised-up that way, it was her mother who was from Iceland. When I was small, I lived where the winters were long, and the winters were for story-telling close to the fire."

"And your father?"

"He was from the Isle of Man, born a fisherman and a sailor on the deep waters. We had no books, so it was stories we told to one another, and I miss hearin' those old yarns."

"I am not a story-teller," she said, "but often I read stories to Peg. You're welcome to listen."

"I'll do that." He paused. "Sometimes I think there were only a few stories and men told them over and over until the names were changed and the places. Maybe all the same stories are told in all the lands. I know I've heard an Injun tell stories of Indians that were the same as those I knew."

"The Isle of Man? Then you're a Manxman."

"Maybe. I wouldn't know where to look even if I had a map. Pa said it was somewhere off the west coast of Scotland."

"Some night soon, we will read, and we will not wait for winter to come to tell our stories."

The stages came and went, and watching the hills and the trees became a habit. Someday a man would come, and with luck she would see him first. What would she do? What could she do?

The navy pistol she kept close at hand. One of the derringers was always with her. Each of them had two barrels.

Two shots, and she must be close.

Temple Boone came and went; sometimes, almost without her knowing, he was there and then he was gone. He talked but little, although occasionally there was news. The station at Virginia Dale had been attacked by Indians, a quick, sharp raid. They were there and gone before it was realized, but they drove off the horses, and the stage had to come on to the next station using the same tired horses.

"Don't get caught outside," Boone warned her. "Get in. Sometimes a shot or two will drive them off. Indians want to steal horses, but they don't want to get killed. They might come at any time, but they prefer an attack at daybreak. Usually, there's just a small bunch of them."

Only a week later, the stage came rolling in on a dead run, and when it drew up at the station, Wilbur dropped to the ground. "Wounded man inside. Injuns shot at us tryin' to stop the stage. We outrun 'em, but they nailed a passenger."

There were five in the stage, and three had joined the shooting at the Indians, helping to drive them off. The wounded man was a soldier in uniform. "Headed for Fort Collins," he explained as he was helped inside. "I don't figure I'm hit hard, but I'm losin' blood." Mary was working on his shoulder, trying to stop the flow of blood when suddenly he looked at her and said, "You're Major Breydon's wife! From Virginia!"

She turned her eyes to his. He was a stocky, well set up man of perhaps forty years. She remembered him at once.

"Sergeant Owen? Barry Owen?"

"Yes, ma'am. I was captured and exchanged on a promise not to fight again in that war, so they sent me out to the frontier. Is the major here?"

"No, sergeant, he was shot, killed."

"Oh? I am sorry, ma'am. I didn't know."

She finished binding his wound. Shakily, he got to his feet. "I am reporting for duty at Fort Collins, ma'am. Maybe I'll get by again."

It was not until the stage was gone that she remembered.

Sgt. Barry Owen had been among those who pursued Flandrau's guerrillas!

But who would know that? Who would guess? Had he ever seen Flandrau? Would he know him if he saw him? Or . . . worse . . . would Flandrau recognize him?

ELEVEN

The days were long and hard. There were times at night when she fell into bed exhausted. There were meals to be prepared, the horses to be cared for, and always they were cleaning. Dust settled on everything, and there were times when she almost found herself sympathizing with Scant Luther and the filth in which he had lived. It would have been so easy just to sit down and let the days drift by.

Yet there were compensations, too. Matty never complained. She did her share of the work and a little more, she bantered with the passengers and the drivers, she teased, cajoled, and made a fuss over Wat until he finally began to loosen up, yet even then he said nothing of his family, nothing of where he had lived before. One thing he denied vehemently. His father was no outlaw and never had been.

Sometimes at night, she longed for the great four-poster in which she had slept at home. She yearned for a quiet afternoon drinking tea with occasional visitors from Washington and the gatherings at her home when officials from Washington mingled with planters from Virginia and occasional travelers from

83

Europe. The beautiful gowns, the uniforms, the music, and the conversation.

Often, she paused in her work and looked with dismay at her hands, once so soft and white, her nails perfect. Now her hands were brown, and there were calluses. Could she ever make them beautiful again?

Most of all, she thought about Peg. What kind of a future would there be for her here? Of course, they still owned the land in Virginia. Battles had been fought over that land, the buildings burned, the stock driven off. It would cost many thousands of dollars to put it in a producing condition and to restock it. Certainly, more than she could earn here running a stage station.

Yet somehow it must be done. She wanted for Peg the graceful, gracious, pleasant life she had known when her father was alive and before the war had torn their lives to shreds.

"Matty," she said suddenly, "when spring comes, we must plant some flowers. I miss them so!"

"And I, mum. Last night, I was thinkin' back to Ireland again."

Mary laughed. "And I to Virginia! Well, it does no harm to remember. Often I worry about Peg. I am afraid her life is so barren here."

" 'Tis no such thing, mum. She'll see more kinds of folks here than ever she'd see elsewhere!"

"Like the Mormon man who wanted you for his second wife?" she said, teasing.

Matty flushed. "Ah, he'd no such thought, mum. He was but teasing, as you are now. But he had a nice smile, a smile from the heart, it was. A girl can always make do with a man who smiles from the heart, mum."

Matty paused, putting down the cup she was drying. "Have you noticed Wat, mum? He's taken to combing his hair before meals, and he washes his hands clean before drying them on the towel."

Mary had been too busy to be lonely, and only occasionally did she stop to remember that life so suddenly gone that it seemed like a dream, like an enchanted time, as indeed it had been.

For all of that, what she did here was useful. It was essential, and *she* was essential. Had she been that back in Virginia? She might have become so, but when all went to pieces back there, she was but another pretty young lady with pretty gowns and a lot of would-be beaus attracted by her father's plantation, perhaps, as much as by her.

"It's useful work, Matty." She voiced her thoughts suddenly. "What we're doing here can be important. These are busy people, but they are often lonely people, too. They are making a long, hard trip, and many of them have no idea what to expect at the end of it. We can leave them with a bright, happy memory, and we can give them a friendly welcome when they come."

" 'Tis my thought exactly, mum. Travelers are either lonely folk, all by themselves, like, or they are herded about like cattle, and a kind word is remembered long after."

"We must have a word for each one if we can, Matty, and we must remember those who come again, as some will. It is flattering to be remembered and called by name."

"Aye." Matty swept a hand around. "We've changed it, mum. It was a dull, dirty room when we came, but now, with the tableclothes, curtains, and all, it's a cheerful room. It's a happy room."

"And clean," Mary agreed.

Mentally, she checked over the stage station, the corrals, the barn, the house. All had been swept, mopped, and cleaned. In the barns, the harness was neatly hung, as in her father's stable. The stalls were clean, and there was fresh hay scattered on the dirt floor in place of the straw they did not have.

Tables had been set outside, ready for the incoming passengers, and inside, about the stove and the fireplace, pots were polished and neatly hung. It was a far different place from what they had come upon first.

Peg and Wat had helped, but much had been done by Ridge Fenton, the hostler she hired from Laporte. Grudgingly, at first, because he detested working for a woman, then with more enthusiasm, he accepted her way of doing things.

"Mr. Fenton," she had said, "you may not like my way of doing things at first, but you are a reasonable man, a man of good judgment and discrimination. Let's try it my way, and then if it does not work, we can always try another."

She paused and then said, "Mr. Fenton, I understand you are from Virginia?"

"West Virginny, ma'am."

"Did you ever get down to Virginia?"

"I did, ma'am, a time or two with my pappy. He taken me to see the capital city one time. Gran'pappy fit in the Revolution, and he wanted me to see what come of it and to see Mr. Jefferson's home and Mount Vernon."

"And did you not pass by a plantation named the Harlequin Oaks?"

"Surely did, ma'am. One o' the finest places in Virginny. My pappy stopped by there to show me the horses runnin' in the pastures behind those whitewashed rail fences and all. Some of the finest stock I ever did see."

"Harlequin Oaks was my home, Mr. Fenton. My father owned it, and the first of my family settled there in 1660."

Ridge Fenton took the pipe from his mouth. He was badly flustered. "Ma'am? You mean, you—"

"It was destroyed in the first year of the war, Mr. Fenton. Someday I hope to return and rebuild it as it was, but for the present I must work, make a home for my daughter, and we must survive, Mr. Fenton. My father taught me to be a survivor."

"Well, I'll be—beggin' your pardon, ma'am. I'd no idea."

"It doesn't matter, Mr. Fenton. All that is past. Whatever there was at Harlequin Oaks was built by my ancestors. Whatever I have here I must build myself, with your help. And I shall very much need your help, Mr. Fenton. When I first arrived, I had some foolish notion that I must do it all myself, to prove myself. I now realize it cannot be done by one person. You are an experienced man, and Mr. Boone has said you are the best stock tender and blacksmith around. I shall value any suggestions you have to make."

"Thanky, ma'am. I'll do what I can."

"Please do, and if you see something that needs doing, that your experience tells you should be done, do not hesitate."

Jason Flandrau . . . she had almost forgotten him, and to forget him even for a minute was a risk. He was somewhere about, and his entire career, even his life, was at stake.

Nevertheless, that was her affair. It was not the business of the Overland Stage Company or of Mark Stacy or anyone but herself. Nor must she permit it to interfere with what must be done at Cherokee Station.

Each morning after the first stage had departed, she made a brief tour of inspection of the stables, the corrals, and the horses available.

There had been Indian raids on several of the stations, and their horses were stolen. If that happened at Cherokee, as sooner or later, it must, what would she do? What could she do?

First, to survive the raid. Second, to get on with the business of the stage company.

She was thinking of that when Temple Boone rode in. "Mr. Boone, I was wondering what might be done if Indians run off with my horses?"

"Be thankful you're alive." He stepped down from the saddle. "You got some coffee on?"

"I do, and you're welcome, but what about the next stage?"

"Unless you can conjure up some horses, they'd have to go on with a tired team." He paused. "The nearest ranch with any extra stock is Preston Collier's place. Have you met him?"

"I have not."

"He runs several hundred head of stock over there. Got himself a big, mighty beautiful house. White columns and all. He's also got a wife and two snooty daughters. Pretty girls, but to me pretty is as pretty does, and they don't do much but go to parties, balls, and teas."

"What is he like?"

"Collier? He's a decent enough man, active in politics, ranching, gold mining, and such. Spends a lot of time in Denver. He's a rich man who keeps busy gettin' richer, but he's straight. He'll have no truck with trickery or double-dealin'. He sets store by his horses, won't have them misused. Any stock tender who gets rough with his horses gets his walkin' papers."

"Would he lend me horses if I needed them?"

Boone shrugged. "Ma'am, that would be between you and Collier. I know he refused Scant Luther, refused him point blank, and ordered him off the place.

"Him and Ben Holladay butted heads a few times, so he's got no use for the stage company. Never rides it, either. Has his own teams and drivers, as you'd guess.

"He must have eight or ten coaches and surreys, and sometimes, when he has folks visitin', they go for picnics back in the hills with servants in white coats to serve 'em. You've never seen the like.

"Everybody who comes from back East seems to head toward his home. Most times he has three or four visitors there, politicians, army officers, European noblemen huntin' big game, that sort of thing. But aside from bein' bullheaded about anything of Ben Holladay's, he's a reasonable man."

"Then if I needed horses, it wouldn't be much help to talk to him?"

"I'd advise you to forget it, ma'am. Even if you got to see him, the fact that you work for Ben would be against you."

When they were seated over coffee, he asked casually, "Had any visitors lately? Men ridin' alone?"

Apprehension was her first feeling. Keeping her voice calm, she said, "No, not really. Should I have?"

He drank some coffee. "Saw some tracks on the trail, but they turned off just before they came in sight of the station. Seems the rider took to the hills, and a thing like that makes me curious. So I sort of follered them. Seems like he scouted around in the brush and trees up yonder, like he was lookin' for a good spot to watch the station."

"An Indian?"

"He was ridin' a shod horse, ma'am, and that usually spells white man, although an Indian ridin' a stole horse might have one that's shod. I'd bet on it this was a white man."

"Did he find the place he wanted? If so, could I see it from here?"

"You couldn't see it, but if you look up there, you can see that tree, the last one in the row? He'll be somewhere right at the base of that tree, maybe restin' his rifle on the stub of a broken branch or somethin'."

Casually, she looked around, located the tree. "How far would you say? One hundred and fifty yards?"

"You're a good judge of distance. I'd guess that would be right close."

"My father taught me to shoot a rifle and shotgun. He used to take me hunting."

"Ever kill anything?"

"A deer . . . I cried."

Boone smiled. "Man's a predator. He's a hunter by instinct. I suspect he's taken his livin' from the wild animals and plants as long as he's been around. But he was a hunter first, bred to be a hunter."

"I don't believe that."

"I didn't suspect you did. But think on it. All the predators have their eyes lookin' forward to keep their eyes on the hunted. The game that's hunted has eyes on the side of their head so they can watch better. You take notice, ma'am, the wolf, the lion, the bear, all animals that hunt others have eyes lookin' straight forward. So does man."

"I don't like to think of that. I hope we've gone beyond such attitudes. Isn't that what civilization does, Mr. Boone? To teach us to live together in peace?"

"I reckon that's the ideal, ma'am, but all folks don't become civilized to onct. There's some of us lag behind, some of us have to protect the rest of you civilized folks from those who haven't gotten beyond the huntin' stage. When a man comes at you with a gun or a knife or a spear, you don't have much time to convince him that he's actin' uncivilized, and he isn't likely to listen. That's when you yourself become uncivilized in a hurry or you die."

"I wouldn't want to kill a man."

"No decent-minded person does, but if there's somebody up on that ridge with a rifle who is about to kill Peg's mother, you'd better kill him first.

"You see, ma'am, when a man sets out to rob and kill, he's strikin' a blow not only at you, at Peg, Wat, and Matty here but at all civilization. He's striking a blow at all man has done to rise from savagery.

"I'm not a scholar, but the way I see it is that men have learned to become what we call civilized men by stages, and every child growing up retraces that pattern during his lifetime.

"There's a time when youngsters like to play capture games, a time when they like to build play houses and huts, if it is only to put a blanket over a couple of chairs and crawl under it.

"There's a time when they like to make bows and arrows, dodging around and hunting each other. Hide-an'-seek is one way of doing it. After a while, he grows beyond that stage, or most of them do.

"Some folks just lag behind. They never grow beyond that hunting and hiding stage. They become thieves and robbers.

"Only a few years ago, a young man could go to war, and if he did enough looting or captured enough horses or arms, he could come home a rich man. Most of those who originally had titles over there in Europe had them because they were especially good at killing and robbing and were given titles for doing it in support of their king.

"Well, we've outgrown that. Or some of us have. The others are still lingering back there in a hunting, gathering, and raiding stage, and if you meet one of them alone in the dark, you'd better remember he's not a human being but a savage, a wild animal, and will act like one."

"So I must descend to his level?"

"If you want to be civilized, ma'am, you're going to have to fight to protect it, or all the civilized will be dead, and we will be back in the darkness of savagery."

"You sound like a philosopher, Mr. Boone."

"No, ma'am, but out there in the night, sometimes with a campfire, a man has time to think. He can't get his thoughts from books. He has to think things out for himself, and a man likes to understand what life he's living and why he must do some things.

"I'm not sure all my thoughts are right. Some of them need a lot more thinking, but you don't try to reason with a man who is trying to kill you, or else you will be dead, and violence will have won another victory over peace.

"You take that man who shot your husband, ma'am. He did it because he saw your husband as a threat to him, and when he tries to kill you, it will be for the same reason.

"Are you goin' to let him do it?"

TWELVE

"What can I do?" She gestured. "I have my work to do, and I must move around a good bit. I have to be outside part of the time."

"First thing, ma'am, this Flandrau feller who you think wants you dead wouldn't want it tied to him. He'll try to send somebody to do the job who isn't close to him but somebody who knows his business.

"That makes it unlikely that he will take a shot at you when the stage is in with folks milling about. Remember, I said it is unlikely, but he *might*. If he's smart, as I believe, he will try to catch you alone in the yard where there's nobody around to see where the shot came from or to start hunting him.

"He would like to slip in here, kill you, and get away clean. If he handles it right, that is just what he will do."

"You don't give me much of a chance."

"No, ma'am, not unless you use your head. Don't walk across the yard alone in broad daylight. Don't establish any habits. That's what he will be looking for. If you go to the stables at a certain hour each morning, he'll be waiting."

She watched him as he walked away. Who *was* he? What

was he? He was said to be good with a gun, and there was a whisper around that he was a very dangerous man. To her, he seemed merely a quiet, still-faced man who rarely smiled but who went about his business with a cool assurance.

What he felt about her or thought of her, she had no idea, yet he had never once suggested this was not her kind of work or that she should get out of this business, as many others had.

She preferred it that way, yet it nettled her a little, also. Thinking of it, she laughed at herself for being so feminine. He was, after all, a very attractive man.

Her eyes strayed toward the tree, and from the corners of her eyes she studied it. Slowly, then, her eyes swept the yard. Of course, that might not be the position the gunman would take up, but if he did, what places in the yard were beyond his vision?

She could go from here around the corral to the back of the barn, or she could go from her house to the blacksmith shop without exposing herself to what might be his firing position.

Her father had served in the Blackhawk War, and there were times when he and her husband would talk for hours about tactics, firing positions, and the ranges of various weapons. She wished she had paid more attention, but who would have guessed she would find herself in such a position as she now held?

In the back room on Larimer Street in Denver, Jason Flandrau sat tipped back in a chair, his boots on the table. "She's there," he said. "You boys saw the wrong woman."

"She was Irish as Paddy's Pig, the one we saw," Turkey Joe Longman said.

"She doesn't count. It's the other one we want. If she's still around when I run for office, she will talk even if she doesn't say something before that."

"Does she know your name?"

"I've no idea, but she's seen me; she saw me right out in the open. I tried to get her then, but she slipped away, God knows how." He swore softly. "Who would ever think she'd show up out here? Of all places?"

"It ain't like back East," Longman said. "You can shoot a man, and nobody blinks. But you even bump into a woman on the street, and you might get hung. I don't like it, Colonel. I don't like it at all."

"Neither do I. Nor do I want to see you hang, which will surely happen if they find out who you are. Or who I am." He took his boots from the table and turned in his chair. "Indians, that's the answer. Run off the horses and kill her while it's being done. Round up a few bad Indians and let them have the horses. In the process, she gets killed, and they are blamed."

"I still don't like it."

Irritated, Flandrau turned on him. "Have you got a better plan? You said yourself you're not getting much of a chance at a shot out there."

"Let me try it a few more days."

"All right. You've always done what you set out to do. But be careful. Be very, very careful. And tell nobody, even our own boys, what you're doing."

When Longman was gone, he ordered a glass of wine and remained at the table. Returning to Laporte was out of the question when there was a possibility she might see him. Did she realize it was he who killed her husband?

The trouble lay with Preston Collier. He needed Collier's support if he planned on running for office, and to reach Collier's place he almost had to go through Laporte and then past Cherokee to Collier's ranch. He could circle around, of course.

If Longman could get rid of Mrs. Breydon, then he would get rid of Longman. He wanted nobody alive who could point a finger at him.

He got to his feet and flicked some dust from his boots with the end of his handkerchief. Carefully, he straightened his cravat. Anyway, it was time he cut himself free from all of the old crowd. His future was assured, and he was moving in a different direction now and needed them no longer. He went out the back door, closing it carefully behind him.

* * *

Longman avoided the trail to Cherokee, staying in the back country away from the traveled road. He held to the rolling hills and the grasslands, a route he had used before. Jason was right, of course. Her testimony could get them hung. Neither the North nor the South had any use for guerrillas. Nonetheless, he was tired of doing Jason's dirty work. It wasn't as if he had never killed a woman, for he had killed a dozen or more in raids, but this was different. He had been one of many then, robbing, killing, and raping without discrimination. Now he was alone, going out to shoot a woman with the necessity of escaping afterward and no friends to fight off his pursuers.

One last time, and he had the spot picked. Move in, await his chance, one clean shot, and a fast getaway. He had even planned that, with a spare horse hidden in a brush corral in the woods.

The sorrel horse he left in the brush corral was a fine animal, and he was fast. He was also a horse Turkey Joe had never been seen riding. A true beauty, the sorrel was, a horse to take the eye of any man who loved or wanted a fast horse.

Turkey Joe rode a gray horse to the line of trees and tied the horse with a slip knot to some brush right behind him. He slid his rifle from the boot and edged up to the tree where he had found a convenient rest for his rifle over the stub of a broken branch. Then he settled down to wait. Turkey Joe Longman had planned carefully and well. The trouble was that, like many another criminal, he had not considered the imponderables, the accidental, the unexpected.

Mary Breydon came to the door with her Henry rifle and placed it beside the door as she had been doing for the past three days. A dozen times in those three days, she had taken up the rifle and aimed it through the brush and trees at the tree Boone had indicated. Her chances of shooting through all that brush without the bullet being deflected were slight, but at least she could, if still alive, strike back.

She had been thinking a good deal about Temple Boone's comments and had decided he was probably right. If civilization was to endure, those who believed in it must be prepared to strike back at the dark forces that would destroy it. Aside from that, she was Peg's mother, and Peg's mother had to live to ensure Peg of the education and the chance she should have. For that, she was willing to fight. She poured a cup of hot coffee.

The stage would be coming soon. She took her apron from the back of a chair and walked to the door, tying it. She had just stepped into the door when, on the hill beyond the trees, Turkey Joe Longman leveled his rifle. In the moment Turkey Joe took aim, the first of the imponderables, the accidental, happened.

Peg turned quickly to speak to her mother and knocked over a cup of coffee. It burned her hand, and she screamed, *"Mama!"*

Mary Breydon turned sharply, and the bullet aimed for her heart burned the outside of her left shoulder.

Almost without thinking, she whipped up the Henry and fired at the target for which she had so often aimed. The bullet missed Turkey Joe but it hit the gray horse. Wheeling about, Turkey Joe hit the saddle, whipping the slip knot free as he passed it, and he was off with a jump.

Temple Boone, throwing one quick glance toward the door, seeing Mary on her feet and Matty beside her, hit the saddle running, Ridge Fenton only a jump behind him on another horse.

At the tree, there was blood on the leaves where the horse had been tied, and the two were off on the trail.

Swearing, Turkey Joe spurred the wounded horse.

Within a few miles, the horse began to labor, and Turkey Joe urged it on. His pursuit was behind him but still far enough away, and he had a fresh horse, a fast horse, waiting.

The second of the imponderables, the unexpected, had happened only minutes before. Bear Walker, a Comanche brave, had come upon the brush corral and the sorrel, and Bear Walker had an eye for horse flesh and a picture of himself riding into the village on such a horse. Bear Walker was no laggard but a man of instant decision.

Dust still hung in the air when Turkey Joe, stripping the gear from the bloody gray, stopped, saddle in hand, staring at the open gate in his corral. Behind him, he heard the pound of hoofs. He dropped the saddle and went for his gun.

The gun came up fast, but not fast enough. The last thing he saw was Temple Boone, gun in hand.

"Damn you, Boone! I—!"

"He's had it comin' for a long time," Ridge Fenton said.

"Vary the hours at which you do things. Avoid patterns." He put down his cup and reached for the coffeepot. "Have you talked to Ridge Fenton about this?"

"No."

"You should. Get him in here, soften him up with a piece of pie or a couple of doughnuts because he's a crusty old codger, as you probably know.

"Tell him what's happening. Lay it on the line to him because Ridge makes a great fuss about bein' gun-shy. He'll tell you he wants no part of any fight. He wants no shooting around where he is. He's a peaceful man. He will tell you that, but don't you believe him because that old man has ridden with Indian war parties, he's had hand-to-hand fights with Indians, he's guided army patrols, and he's been fightin' since he was knee-high. Believe me, and I've been around the mountain a few times, I'd rather tackle three cougars in your tack room than that old man when he's riled."

He paused, drawing his cup near. "How about Wat?"

"He knows, but he's just a small boy."

"And a mighty tricky one. Don't you forget that he survived on his own for some little time. He listens a lot, misses mighty little, and he can track better than most grown men."

He finished his coffee and pulled back from the table. "I'll be around time to time. If you need me, Wat will know where I am."

THIRTEEN

Jason Flandrau was at supper in the hotel dining room when
he overheard the conversation.

"Can't figure it out," a man was saying. "Who would want to
shoot a woman? If it had been Scant Luther, I'd not be surprised, but this was a man named Longman. Shot at her from
ambush."

"He ought to be hung!"

"Too late," the first speaker commented. "Temple Boone
caught up with him, and Longman was a little slow."

"What was Longman's connection?"

"That's just it. There is no connection of which anybody
knows. It seems Longman was by the station at Cherokee just a
few days ago, but he didn't see Mrs. Breydon—"

"Breydon? Wasn't that the name of that former army officer
who was shot over at Julesburg a few months ago?"

Jason Flandrau's back was to them, but he felt a sudden
chill. It was getting close, too close. Somebody would be apt to
remember who had done that shooting and wonder if there was
any connection. For a moment, he sat very still, carefully
reviewing his past meetings with Longman.

Had they been seen together? He had tried to be careful, but there had seemed no reason to be too careful until now.

The worst of it was he would have to move with extreme care. If people were already wondering and anything else happened, they would start not only asking questions but looking for the answers.

Should he move out now? Leave Colorado at once, for Montana, perhaps? Or California? That was stupid. He had established himself here. They were talking of him for governor, perhaps for senator. He had been fortunate here and had fallen in with the right group at the right time. Such a coincidence might not happen again. Could he let one woman stand between him and the wealth that could be his by discreetly using his power as governor? And all the honor and position that would be his?

But what to do? His strong right hand was gone. At least he had not talked. Thoughtfully, he began considering the men who were left to him, the men from the old outfit. Most of them were simply brutes, tough, lawless men who were loyal enough as long as they had money to gamble and buy whiskey. They knew him, but none of them were in his confidence.

What about that young fellow, that friend of Turkey Joe's? He was, Longman had said, very good with a gun, and he was shrewd.

Jason Flandrau finished his meal, but he ate without appetite. To attempt to kill Mary Breydon now would be stupid, but he could not afford to let her live.

He got up and walked into the street, standing there, looking about. He reached into his vest pocket and took out his watch, glanced at it, then returned it to his pocket and walked back to his office. Jordy Neff was waiting for him when he stepped in.

"That true what they're sayin' about Joe?"

"It is. Temple Boone killed him."

"Maybe I better go call on Mr. Boone. Turkey Joe was my partner."

"You were out at Cherokee with him? And you only saw one woman?"

"Woman and a boy-kid. It was John Tanner's boy."

"I don't know the name?"

"Owned him a ranch over yonder by Bonnar Springs. West of Owl Canyon. Had a few head of cows, some horses, but his place was a natural hideout, and there was a kind of natural rock fortress there, so some of the boys began usin' it for a hideout.

"Tanner didn't like it much, but there wasn't much he could do. Then, one day, one of the boys hit the kid over some impudence, and Tanner objected. This man—it was Mody Mercer—he damn near beat Tanner to death. Tanner crawled away, and a couple of days later, when he could walk, he came back with a gun. He hadn't much luck that way, either. Mercer killed him. A few days after that, the boy disappeared. Never saw him again until he showed up there at Cherokee."

"This Mercer now? Where's he from?"

"Missouri, or so I heard, but that doesn't mean much because around that time Missouri was a sort of a catch basin for anybody runnin' loose.

"The story was that he rode with Bloody Bill Anderson. He's no gun hand, but he's mean. Shoot you in the back or kill you with an ax . . . anything."

Mody Mercer . . . a name to remember.

"Jordy? Stay away from Boone. Do you hear me?"

Neff stiffened. "Now look here—!"

"Neff, I need a few good men, men who can do what they are told and who know how to keep their mouths shut. I had hoped to have Joe Longman around, but since he can't be, I'd been thinking about you." Flandrau took two gold pieces from his pocket and placed them on the table. "It's a lot easier than punching cows or working in a mine and a lot safer than what that crowd at Bonnar Springs were doing."

Jordy Neff hesitated, thought of the three silver dollars in his pocket, and picked up the gold pieces. "What do I have to do?"

"Just be around, and when I take my watch out of my pocket with my left hand, meet me here, just like today, just like Turkey Joe told you."

Jordy Neff would be useful. He looked like a nice, clean-cut young man, and he was good with a gun. Maybe, in time, he would let him kill Temple Boone.

If he could. Temple Boone was, all agreed, very, very fast.

That was all very good, all very convenient, but the man who interested him was Mody Mercer, and that other man, only now recovered from his wound. The man they called Scant Luther.

Scant was drinking more than he should, and Scant was nursing a grudge.

When the sun went down, Mary Breydon went back inside. Her shoulder was almost healed, although she was still wearing a bandage to cover the wound. It had barely split the skin but had been sore for days and hurt when she forgot and moved her arm too freely.

Turkey Joe Longman, they said his name was, would come no more, but who might be the next one that would be sent?

"It was well planned," Boone commented. "He'd had a horse waiting, but it was stolen before he could reach it. He had no choice but to make a fight."

He paused. "Do not think it was only for you, ma'am. He had attacked from ambush, and if we are to have a good life here, such things cannot be permitted. To have arrested him, had there been an officer present, would only mean that he'd be turned loose. Longman had a friend who would have protected him. However, he gave us no choice. It was kill or be killed."

"Will you have supper with us, Mr. Boone?"

"I will, ma'am, and gladly. Whether it is Matty or yourself who does it, you set the best table in Colorado."

"That's an exaggeration, Mr. Boone, but thank you."

When they were at the table, Peg said, "Mama, tell us about your home. I mean, when you were a little girl."

"I'm afraid Mr. Boone wouldn't want to hear all that. Maybe some other time—"

"On the contrary, ma'am. I'd be most interested."

"All right, I will if Matty will."

"My story would be nothing the like of yours, mum, but if it's my story you would hear, I'll tell it, as much as I can." She paused, cup in hand. "But you first, mum. It is your story we would hear."

"It is all gone now, the house where I was born and where we lived. My grandfather named it Harlequin Oaks when he finished it, and my family had lived there one hundred years before the big house was built.

"The first of us came there in 1660 when it was wilderness. He cut down logs and built a cabin and a barn and plowed land. He chose the site for the big house and cleared the land, leaving the fine big oak trees where they were. He had been an officer in the army, and he brought two of his men with him when he settled, and each of them took land nearby but worked for him.

"By the time I was born, all the building was done. We had fine horses and carriages—"

"Slaves?" Boone asked.

"Never! My ancestor who built the first cabin, he had been captured from a ship by Algerian pirates and had himself been a slave—"

"But he was a white man?"

"Yes, he was, but many whites were enslaved in Algiers, Tunis, and elsewhere. As for that, there had been slaves in Europe for a thousand years before ever they saw a black man.

"The Romans enslaved the Greeks and later the Gauls, the Jews, whoever they conquered. It was so all over the world, I'm told. When they conquered a people, they killed them or made slaves of them.

"My grandfather, though, he said slaves were too expensive. It was cheaper, he said, to hire men to do the work than to feed and clothe them the year around.

"Aside from the house, there were two barns for hay and wheat, four stables for cows, horses, and mules, the carriage house, a smoke house, and an ice house. There was also a walled-in spring.

"The brick for the house was made right on the place, and the lumber was cut there or in the mountains not far away. My great-grandfather and my grandfather supervised the work themselves, just as they did all the planting that was done."

"Were there many rooms?" Wat asked.

"Twenty-eight, I believe, in the main house. As you went in, the study was on the right, and there was a stair to the second floor on the left.

"One could walk straight through to the garden, but on the right of the hall was the parlor, on the left the dining room."

"Quite a place," Boone commented.

"My father loved to entertain, so we often had people staying with us, and on almost any evening we had from four to eight guests. When people traveled by carriage in those days, they often stopped with friends, and of course we had many of those who came up the Shenandoah Valley who were going on to Washington."

"You still have guests," Boone said, "only you have to share them with the Overland Stage Company."

Mary looked up at Matty, who had started to clear the table. "Now it's your turn, Matty."

"Another time," Matty said, "but 'twill be no such tale as yours, nor was I born in a house so grand but in a wee cottage with a thatched roof where we could look westward over the sea." She paused, dishes in hand. "My first memories were of me mother standin' lookin' off to sea, shadin' her eyes for a sight of m' father's boat.

"The sea gave us our livin', such as it was, but we dinna trust it to bring back those who sailed out upon it, and many's the poor lad from the village who sailed after fish and was seen no more, my father among them."

"He was a fisherman?"

"Aye, but a soldier before that. As a lad, he fought in Spain with Wellington and was at Waterloo with a brother of his on the side of Bonaparte. He saved a bit, my father did, and married late and bought the boat, and 'twas a good living we had whilst he lived and before the sea took him, and his boat, too. Only the sea gave us back the boat but not the man."

"On another night you must tell us, Matty." She turned to Boone. "And you, Mr. Boone? You've a story, I am sure. Will we hear it someday?"

He smiled. "What story could I tell? I know little enough of my people, although I've a memory of sitting by a field while my father plowed, the lines about his neck so he could have both hands for the plow. I remember the crops standing tall and my mother crying when the grasshoppers took it all.

"I was a sagebrush orphan like Wat here. Cholera took my mother and father and my baby sister. My father was wanting to cross the plains to Oregon, but he lacked the money. He had six crow-bait cattle hitched to our old farm wagon, but no wagon train would accept him.

"That wagon would break down before you'd gone fifty miles if your stock didn't die first. We can't risk it, they all said, to have the wagon train waiting while you made repairs. It would be a risk for us all."

He pushed back from the table. "They were right, of course. We hadn't supplies enough for the trip. Only pa was figuring on hunting enough to feed us. He hadn't thought how the game would stay away from the wagon trails and he'd see nothing for days.

"Pa was a good hunter, a dead shot with a rifle and a hard worker, but it just wasn't enough. You have to have luck, too, and pa didn't have it. Year after year, I saw him whipped by flood, frost, drouth, and grasshoppers, and always he'd come back and try again."

Long after the last coal-oil light was out, when only embers smoldered on the hearth, when brief flames made the shadows dance on the log walls, Peg whispered, "Mama? If that man had killed you, would I be a sagebrush orphan?"

"He did not kill me, Peg, and he won't."

"But if he had?"

She lay wide-eyed, staring up at the rafters. "Yes, Peg, I am afraid you would."

Later, she said, "Go to sleep, Peg. You'll be all right. Matty would take care of you."

After a long time, Peg whispered again, "And Mr. Boone? And Wat?"

"Yes, Peg. Mr. Boone and Wat, too. Now go to sleep."

FOURTEEN

When morning sent the first gray light through the window, she was up. She went to her purse and carefully counted over what money she had left. She had sold the pearls her father had given her when she became sixteen, sold them to buy their outfit.

Marshall had sold two horses he had managed to keep throughout the war, and they had come West, Marshall first and then Peg and herself. The little money she had was going all too fast, and she could not earn enough here to provide for Peg.

Realistically, she had to think of what would become of Peg if she were killed. People always had an idea such things never happened to them, but she knew otherwise, and it had happened to Marshall, the best, the bravest, the kindest of men.

Looking at the little there was left, she thought of the years before Peg would be a woman. And Wat, she must think of him, too, although he was a solid little fellow, already doing a man's work cheerfully and without question, seemingly glad to just have a home. But Wat was part of the family now.

He was a good boy, she thought, but too tight, too controlled, too reticent. He was learning to share, even wanting to share now that he was one of them.

If only she had some of the dresses she used to give away! If only she had the material, the needles, thread, buttons! It was easy to mend and even to create clothing if one had the things to do with, all of which she had so taken for granted at Harlequin Oaks. She had only to wish and to speak and it was there, ready for her.

Her trunks! Of course, why had she not thought of them! They were in storage at the Brewsters', and she could write for them to be sent. Fortunately, to sew was one thing all young ladies learned. It was one of the things you *did*. Sewing, riding, music, were all considered things a young lady did well, and dancing, of course.

She smiled grimly. Who would have guessed that what served her best now was what her father would have expected from any stableboy! Yet when she walked through the barn and saw how orderly and efficient it all was, she blessed her father over and over again.

The trunks . . . she must send for the trunks. She could remake many of those dresses, some for herself, for Matty, and for Peg.

Matty was kindling a fire as she came out. Matty stood up. "Wat's gone for an armful of wood. Be careful, mum, if you're goin' outside."

"Be sure and save any newspapers, Matty. Sometimes the passengers leave them behind. We know so little of what is happening in the war. Sometimes I feel ashamed, when they are all suffering so."

"We've troubles enough of our own, mum. There's been no papers, although I put by a book of Mr. Dickens's that was left behind, thinkin' the poor man who left it would be comin' for it. I used to read him in the newspapers. Mr. Dickens, I mean."

Matty paused. "You get no letters from home, mum?"

Mary's lips tightened; then she said quietly, "No, Matty. I am from Virginia, and most of my friends are with the South. My husband was a Union Army officer; my father was against secession. I am afraid many of my friends think me a traitor."

"I know little of the war, mum. I'd only just come over when the fighting began. Is it about slavery, then?"

"Not really, although that is a part of it. Mostly, it is about states' rights and whether the state or the nation shall control. I am ashamed to say I know less about it than I should.

"There was much talk about it at home, but I was a young girl, busy with riding, dancing, going to parties. I don't think many of us realized how serious it was until it was too late. All of a sudden, all the young men were in uniform, either blue or gray, and they were riding off to war.

"Some of our old friends did write, but I became irritated, I am afraid. Even when the war was growing worse and worse, there was more talk of promotion and who was getting what command than of the war itself."

She paused. "I am sending East for some trunks I left behind. Maybe there's something in them we can make over."

"Will they still be there, mum? I mean with the fighting and all?"

"I hope so." She hesitated, thinking. She would write to Martha Brewster, but it might be well to write to someone else, someone in authority. She considered that. Yes, yes, of course!

She went outside after a careful look around from the door, then walked around the corral. She must stop that, too. She remembered Temple Boone's warning and something she had heard her father say about avoiding patterns of behavior when fighting Indians, for they quickly grasped the pattern and were waiting for you.

When she had gone through the barn where Ridge Fenton was harnessing the team for the incoming stage, she paused at the door. "Mr. Fenton? Have you heard anything about the war?"

"Not much, ma'am. They're still fightin'." He straightened up, resting a hand on a horse's shoulder. "It's so far away, ma'am, and we got so much to think of out here."

She scanned the hills slowly, deliberately, looking for anything that might suggest the presence of an enemy. She was not very good at it, and she might miss what would be obvious to men like Temple Boone or Ridge Fenton.

She crossed the yard then, her heart pounding. Was it fear she felt? Apprehension?

Once inside, she looked around the station, wondering what might be done to make it more inviting. From the first, she had understood that she could not compete with old, experienced station agents, not at least until she had more on-the-job experience. What she could do was to create a more restful, homelike atmosphere. On the way out from Missouri, she had noticed most of the stations were untidy, and the food was often just thrown on the tables.

She was perfectly aware that Mark Stacy had not made up his mind, and Ben Holladay knew nothing about her at all. She could not be just as good as the others; she had to be a little bit better.

What of Scant Luther? From time to time, she had heard that he was still around, that he was nursing a grudge.

She had turned in the doorway when the first of the carriages came into the yard. Under the coating of dust from the trail, it was black and shining, as were the six horses that drew it. There were a half-dozen men and four women in the carriage laughing and chatting.

A moment later, a second carriage pulled up, and someone leaned out and said, "Why are we stopping? This isn't the ranch!"

"No"—a young man got down from the seat beside the driver—"but it is the last time you will have a chance to get a cup of coffee or tea before we get there. We've miles to go."

"That suits me." A young woman accepted his hand and got down. "Regina? Are you coming?"

"Why don't we wait? This is just a stage station, and their food is awful!"

The young man with the curly hair turned to Mary. "Is that true? Is your food awful?"

She smiled. "Why don't you try it? Our coffee is really very good, and we've tea. Won't you come in?"

"Archie!" Regina called. *"Really!"*

"I am thirsty," Archie said, "and besides that"—he turned to look at Mary again—"she's very pretty!"

One of the other men stepped down, holding his hand to help another young woman down. "He's right, Regina. We are thirsty. Even if it is only a few miles, I'd feel better for something to drink, if it is only water."

"Go in, if you like," Regina said. "I shall be served here."

She turned to look at Mary. "A cup of tea, please."

Mary Breydon smiled. "I am sorry. We only serve at the tables."

"But I am Regina Collier!"

"How nice for you! But we do serve only at the tables."

Regina Collier was angry. Was this stage person being impudent? "I am afraid you do not understand," she said icily. "I am Preston Collier's daughter!"

Mary Breydon smiled. "I understand perfectly, Miss Collier. We are very busy here and do not have time to serve people in carriages or stages." She smiled again. "I could not serve you in your carriage if you were President Lincoln. Of course," she added, "he would not ask me to!"

Turning, she went back to the tables where nine young people had gathered, laughing and talking. Matty was just serving the last of them and had put a platter of cookies on the table.

Archie went back to Regina's carriage. "Come on!" he invited. "The coffee's really very good, and so are the cookies!" He offered his hand.

"No," Regina said stubbornly. "I shall stay here. I will not yield to that—that woman!"

"Oh, come now, Regina! They have their rules, you know! And she's really a very nice woman!"

"You do as you like. I will not be insulted by a common waitress!"

Archie's smile faded. "I am sorry," he said, and returned to the table, joining again in the excited talk.

Mary refilled his cup. "Thank you," he said. "We haven't far to go, but we were all very thirsty. It's a dusty ride."

"I know. You are going to Preston Collier's?"

"Yes, there's a party there, a reception for some chap from England who has come over to hunt and see how the colonials are progressing. He's a nice chap, really, and this is his second trip, although I do not believe he was ever this far west."

"He will enjoy it, I am sure. Is there anything else I can get for you?"

"Not at all, and thank you." Archie hesitated, then said, "I must apologize for Miss Collier."

"Please don't. I am not in the least offended. We all have our bad moments, and no doubt she is tired."

Archie looked at her, somewhat puzzled. "You have not been here long, Miss—?"

"Breydon. Mrs. Mary Breydon."

"Oh? Your husband is here, then?"

"Major Breydon was killed. I am a widow."

"I am sorry. I didn't mean to pry."

"I am sure you did not." She glanced around to see the others drifting back to their carriages. "I hope your weekend is a pleasant one. Now if you will forgive me?" She turned and went back to the table and began gathering the empty cups and the saucers.

He glanced after her, still puzzled, then walked back to the carriage.

"I hope you enjoyed your chat," Regina said irritably.

"I did, indeed," Archie replied. "Your neighbor is a surprising young woman."

"She is *not* my neighbor! This is merely a station on the Overland Stage Line, and I suppose she works for them. We never stop here," she added.

"Is Sir Charles already at the ranch?" he asked, changing the subject.

"Yes, he is. He came down yesterday with father. I believe he wanted to do some shooting this morning. There are always deer, you know, but father says the elk are disappearing. They are going into the high country as the snow goes off."

"He has been here before, you said?"

"Some kind of a diplomatic mission, I believe. He was in

Washington, D.C., before the war began, but it was only for a few weeks."

"I know something about him, but we've never met," Archie commented. "My brother knew him in Paris when they were at school there. For such a young man, he's become quite a famous diplomat. He's been to Cairo, to Constantinople, to Vienna and Rome on missions of some sort or other."

"Father met him in Washington, and when he expressed a wish to hunt, father invited him out."

"Who else will be there?"

"Oh, you know! The usual crowd. The Talbots, the Kings, the Williamses, and some new man whom I've never met, although they say he is both very handsome and very important, a Colonel Flandrau."

"He's been around Denver. I believe he's investing in mines. There are so many new people around now that it's hard to keep up with them. They keep coming and going, investing in mines or cattle or town sites. If it isn't one thing, it's another."

Archie glanced ahead. In the distance, at the end of a winding road, he glimpsed the white columns of the Collier ranch house.

Peg stood in the door watching the carriages go by. Four more passed during the hour, then a fifth. "Where are they all going, mama?"

"Mr. Collier is having some friends down for the weekend, I believe."

"Was it like that at Harlequin Oaks when you were a little girl?"

"Yes, it was, only the country back there is greener, and there were more carriages, and many people rode over on horseback from neighboring places. We lived closer together than people do here."

Temple Boone rode in before noon. "Mrs. Breydon? Better stay close to the station and keep the youngsters inside. There's a report of an Injun raid on a small place east of Virginia Dale."

"But isn't that quite far off?"

"Ma'am, they burned the house and killed two men. They were riding south according to the tracks." He swung his horse. "I'll tell Ridge." He looked back. "You be careful now!"

Indians . . . here?

FIFTEEN

With the rising sun, there was a change in the weather. The sky, which had been clear, clouded over, and there was a spatter of cold rain, then a brief gust of wind that sent the leaves skittering across the hard-packed ground.

Trees bent before the wind, and a loose door banged. Temple Boone, bowing before the wind, came from the barn, closing the door behind him.

When he reached the station, he said, "Looks like a storm coming." There was another brief spatter of rain that ceased abruptly.

"Where is Ridge?" Matty asked. "Is he all right, then?"

"He's in the barn, ma'am, and you know Ridge. He'll sleep there." Boone rested his rifle against the wall near the window. "Saw some tracks out yonder a few hours ago. Pony tracks."

"Indians?"

"Sioux, I'd guess, and that means trouble."

"Where is Wat?" Peg asked.

"He'll stay in the tack room. He'll be with Ridge, and they'll take turns watchin'. That lad's as good as any man when it comes to that."

113

He held his hands to the fire. "Wind's cold," he said. "Uncommon for this time of year."

"Will it be safe for the stages?" Peg asked. "Won't they have to stop?"

"Stages don't stop for nothin', Peg," Boone said. "They carry mail, and they have to keep movin'. Most of the passengers would prefer to keep goin', too."

He added fuel to the fire and edged the coffeepot farther over to heat the coffee. "I came by Preston Collier's and stopped off to warn them. They'd had the news, but they don't seem worried. Must be forty or fifty people over there to meet that English lord."

"He isn't really a lord, is he, mama? Isn't a 'sir' just a knight?"

"You're right, Peg. So many Americans think anyone with a title such as 'count' or 'earl' is royalty. It isn't true. Only members of a royal family are royalty. The others belong to the nobility."

"Never set much store on such things," Boone commented. "A man should be two things. He should be a man, and he should be a gentleman. I mean a gentleman in his behavior. That's the way I was raised."

"How does one become an earl or a count?" Peg asked.

"Usually, from service to his king. Once it was a reward for bravery or skill in battle, then for other services to the king. Usually, with the title went a grant of land, and the nobleman was expected to respond on call with a certain number of soldiers to serve his king during a war.

"Such titles were often passed down from father to son or occasionally to a near relative, always with the expectation of service to the king. Some of the noblemen became so powerful they threatened the power of the king himself. Others had their estates and titles taken from them and given to others.

"Nowadays, a title is often given for other services, even for diplomatic or business successes, and the titles vary in importance according to the country where they are given."

There was a brief roll of thunder, then, after a moment, a flash of distant lightning.

"You won't have many travelers in this kind of weather,"

Boone said. "Probably nobody until the stage comes by in the morning."

He finished his coffee. "I've got to ride on over to Fort Collins," he explained. "I should be back before daybreak. I'm carryin' dispatches for the army." He glanced over at Mary. "Will you be all right here?"

"Of course. You've no cause to worry about us. Ridge is here, and we're armed."

"I've never seen a red Indian," Matty said, "except that old man who came through on the stage. He seemed a fine old man."

Boone chuckled. "Him? You just bet he is a fine old man, but in his day he was a holy terror. He was a Ute. They are mountain Indians, properly speakin', and he's probably taken thirty or forty scalps in his time."

"That nice old man?" Mary exclaimed. "He had such an amused expression on his face."

"He probably was amused," Boone said. "He was probably thinkin' how silly some of our ways are, compared to his. Every people seems to think their way is the best, and maybe it is, for them."

Temple Boone took his rifle, paused a moment at the door, glanced back at Mary, and lifted his hand. Then he went outside.

"I'd better get in another armful of wood," Matty said. "It will be a cold night."

As she was going out, they heard the clatter of horse's hoofs, and Temple Boone was gone. "I wish he had stayed," Peg said. "I feel safer when he's here."

"We all do," her mother said, "but he has his work to do."

She glanced out the window. There were six horses in the corral huddled together against the wind. For a moment, she hesitated. Should she have them put in the barn? With Ridge's saddle horse, there was scarcely room for them all, and they did not have to be harnessed until morning. There was hay in the corral, and these were mustangs, bred to the wild, unused to barns.

"Come on, Matty, we'll fix supper, and then I'll read a bit to you all. It's a good night to be inside."

She went to the window again and looked out. Nothing

moved. From old habit, her eyes scanned the trees and the brush. The thought of Indians worried her, but she did not want to frighten Peg.

Had she been wrong to bring a child to this wild country? Or to come herself?

No. It had been their only chance, and when spring came, she would find a place and file on some land herself.

Why not? She could prove up on a homestead as well as anyone, and it would be one more thing Peg would have if anything happened to her.

"You should file on a homestead, Matty," she said suddenly. "There's nothing like owning land."

"How much could I get, then?"

"One hundred and sixty acres, but you have to build a shack, sink a well, and plow some land."

"One hundred and sixty acres!" Matty was aghast. "It is a rich woman I'd be!"

"Not quite that, Matty, but it is something for yourself, something that would belong to you."

"We'd better fix supper," Matty said. "Mr. Fenton will be hungry."

"I'm hungry, too!" Peg declared.

"The light is fading," Mary said. "What there is of it!"

Suddenly, even as she watched, the corral gate swung open as if of its own volition. She started. "Why somebody must have—!"

There was a shrill whoop, and then the horses came stampeding from the corral, a running Indian behind them. Ridge Fenton's old buffalo gun boomed from the barn, and she saw a dozen mounted Indians come sweeping around the corral and from behind the barn and take in after the stage horses. One of the Indians was clinging to his horse, blood streaming from a wound and turning the side of his horse crimson.

"Matty!" she cried. "They are stealing our horses!"

She caught up her rifle and, without thinking, threw open the door and fired. She saw an Indian turn his head toward her, and he waved at her derisively, then was gone. She fired again, too late.

Slowly, she lowered her rifle. She had failed. The horses were gone. What was she to do?

Peg was staring at her, round-eyed. "You shot at them? Did you hit one?"

"I don't think so, Peg. I missed. And the horses are gone—gone! When the stage comes in the morning—!"

Ridge Fenton, rifle in hand, came in from the barn. "Sorry, ma'am, they was on us afore I realized. Must've been a dozen of them, right out of nowhere!"

"It wasn't your fault, Mr. Fenton. At least you wounded one of them."

"No, ma'am," Ridge said, "I killed him. Any time a man bleeds like that, he's a goner. Make 'em more careful next time. But don't you worry, ma'am. Those Injuns know who done it. They know better than to try an' steal hosses when I'm around."

"But they did get the horses, Mr. Fenton, and we have a stage coming in tomorrow morning."

"Nothin' we can do, ma'am, until Stacy gets us some more hosses."

"Doesn't Mr. Collier have horses?" Matty asked. "If you were to ask—?"

"Wouldn't give you the time o' day!" Fenton said. "He's got no use for Ben Holladay. Never did have. Them two just don't get along. Too much alike, I reckon."

Mary Breydon took off her apron. "Nevertheless, I'm going to try! I don't want people saying that if a man had been running this station, it wouldn't have happened. I'm going over there."

"Ma'am, it's coming on to storm, and there's Injuns about. You just set down, an'—"

"Mr. Fenton, you take care of things here. And if you would let me, I'd like to borrow your horse."

"Now see here, ma'am! That there's a mighty uneasy animal! He don't take to women no way, and he doesn't like other folks ridin' him."

"Are you saying I can't have him?"

Fenton looked right and left. He rubbed his jaw, glanced

sheepishly at her, and cleared his throat. "No, ma'am, it ain't that. I jest—"

"Thank you, Mr. Fenton. I'll get my cape."

Ridge started to speak, then muttered angrily about "fool woman!" and started off toward the barn.

Matty stared at her. "Ma'am? Do you think you should? There's Indians and all, and Peg here—she's already lost her daddy."

"I have a job to do, Matty. Don't worry. I ride very well, and I shall be back before you realize it. Just you stay inside and keep Peg in."

Ridge was holding his horse at the door. He had saddled it with her sidesaddle. "Don't know how you ride one of them durned things!" he protested. "Moreover, I don't think Arthur will stand for it."

"Arthur? You call him *Arthur?*"

"He was give to me by a man named Arthur, so I just got to callin' him that Arthur horse, and it sort of worked itself down to just Arthur."

She walked up to the horse and put a hand on his neck. "Hello, Arthur. We're going to be friends, aren't we?"

Arthur rolled a wary eye at her but did not seem displeased at the soft touch on his neck. Accepting a hand from Fenton, she mounted quickly. Arthur shied at the unfamiliar feel of the skirt against his flank and the different weight, but he recognized an authoritative, knowing hand on the reins.

The night had grown colder; the sky was still overcast. Arthur seemed ready to go, so she let him have his head. She wore the heavy pistol under her coat and had both derringers in pockets in the rough skirt she was wearing.

Indians . . .

They could be anywhere! Suddenly, and for the first time, she was frightened. What in the world had possessed her that she would start off in the middle of the night . . . but it really wasn't that late, scarcely more than nine o'clock.

The risk had not entered her mind. Not really. All she thought of was that stage coming in, the horses weary from the long run, another run ahead of them.

She had to have a fresh team. Whose was the responsibility

if not hers? She did not ask herself what Scant Luther would have done or Mark Stacy or Boone. She thought only of what she must do.

The horse's hoofs pounded on the hard road. The rain had no more than settled the dust. Wind tore at her clothes and lashed the brush into weird shapes. She slowed Arthur, not wanting him to run himself out. She had heard that mustangs could run on and on, but she was accustomed to the finely bred horses of Virginia and Maryland.

Arthur slowed at her urging, but he was perfectly prepared to keep running. She patted his neck and talked to him, and he cocked a surprised ear at her and kept going.

Again, it started to rain, a quick flurry of hard-driven drops, cold as ice. It stung on her flesh and slapped at her cape like angry fingers.

Suddenly, Arthur shied, snorted, and something moved in the woods alongside the trail. Mary reached under the cape and put her fingers around the butt of the pistol.

Arthur kept going. Whatever was back there was something he did not like, but he was not about to be stopped by it.

She rode into the open, and there, atop the knoll before them, was the house, ablaze with lights, lights that reflected on the glistening, varnished sides of the carriages. She rode on, weaving through the carriages to the white railing of the hitching posts. Dismounting, she tied Arthur and ran up the steps.

At the doorway, she paused, throwing her cape off her hair. A surprised butler, a black man, turned to her. "Yes, miss? Was there something?"

"May I see Mr. Collier, please? It is quite important."

"Are you a guest, miss?" He noticed her muddy boots and beyond her the cow pony tied at the rail. "I see you are not."

He was politely apologetic. "You see, ma'am, Mr. Collier does not like to be disturbed when he is with his guests."

"It is really very important, and I have ridden a long way—"

The door was open, and she could see them dancing within. They were playing a waltz, and she was not a guest; she was an outsider. For a moment, she started to turn away; then her lips tightened.

"Will you take me to him, please? Or ask him to see me?"

Something in her voice made him look at her again. Not only her voice but her manner.

"Certainly, miss, I shall see what I can do."

Suddenly, several couples came out on the wide veranda. One of them was Regina Collier. "What is it, Richard?"

"It's a young lady, Miss Regina. She wishes to speak to your father."

Regina looked past Richard, and her eyes met Mary's. "Oh, it's not important, Richard. It's just that woman from the stage station. If it is important, father can stop by there in the morning."

Mary stepped forward into the light. "Please, Miss Collier, it is very important. Could I see him now?"

What she might have answered, Mary had no idea. Suddenly, there was a cry from the doorway. A tall man in the uniform of a British officer started toward her.

"Mary! Mary Claybourne! Of all people! What in the world are *you* doing *here!*"

SIXTEEN

"Sir Charles!" She held out both hands to him. "You are the one who should answer that question! What are *you* doing here?"

"I came to hunt buffalo," he said, "and Preston was kind enough to invite me to stay with him." He glanced at her clothing. "But, Mary? You haven't come to the party?"

"I'm afraid not, Charles. Harlequin Oaks was destroyed early in the war, our horses were stolen, and my father died just before the war.

"I married Major Marshall Breydon. Do you remember him? The plantation was destroyed, and there was nothing for us to do but find another way to earn a living until the war was over. The land is still mine, of course, but in the meanwhile, I'm operating a stage station."

He laughed. "But that is charming! You, Mary Claybourne, a station agent?" He laughed again. "Only in America!"

Several of the guests had come to the door, and Mary was suddenly self-conscious. "Really, Charles, I just came to see Preston Collier. It is something of an emergency."

"You know him, of course?"

"No, we've never met. I've been here such a short time."

"Mary, I will find him for you, but first you must dance with me!"

"Dance? Here, now? Oh, no! I am not a guest, Charles, and I am not dressed for—"

"You are my guest! I insist, for old times' sake!"

The musicians were playing another waltz. Suddenly, she laughed. "Why not, Charles? I'd love to!"

On the wide veranda, with a light rain falling outside and the other guests watching from the doorways, she danced, muddy boots and all. Suddenly, she felt gay, happy. . . . It was like old times!

For the moment, all was forgotten, only the music, an old friend from far off, better times, and the steps of the waltz. She had always loved to dance, and Sir Charles was a marvelous dancer. Carried away, she danced as she had not danced in years, and when they stopped, there was a brief spattering of applause.

Preston Collier came up to them. "Sir Charles? Please present me. I am afraid I have not had the pleasure."

"Preston, this is Mary Claybourne. I mean, Mrs. Mary Breydon. She is an old, old friend from Virginia! Many times when I was in Washington, she and her family entertained me in their home, at Harlequin Oaks.

"They were the most beautiful parties, and I spent many, many happy hours in her home! Her father was alive then, and he was a remarkable man. Remarkable in every way. Besides that, he had the finest horses I've ever ridden.

"I just couldn't believe it when I saw her here, of all places."

"This is a pleasure, Mrs. Breydon. Won't you join us?"

"Thank you, Mr. Collier, but I am not dressed for it, nor do I, unfortunately, have the time. As a matter of fact, I rode over here in a great hurry to see you on business."

"Business?"

"I am the station agent at Cherokee now, Mr. Collier, and we've just experienced an Indian raid. Nobody was injured unless it was one Indian, but they drove off our horses."

"So? I am sorry, but I do not understand."

"I was hoping to borrow six horses from you so the morning stage could leave on time."

Collier was embarrassed, and suddenly Mary felt sorry for him. It was unfair to make the request in the presence of a guest, but—

"I know you are not friendly with Ben Holladay, Mr. Collier, but would you lend the horses to me personally? After the one round trip, I shall return them to you."

"Mrs. Breydon," Collier said suddenly, "I sincerely regret that we have not met before. I am afraid that the loss is ours, and you may be sure we will make amends for the oversight.

"As to the horses, I shall instruct Burke to deliver them to you at once. The morning stage, you say?"

"Yes, and thank you, Mr. Collier."

"Say no more." He glanced around. "Will you join me in my study for coffee? It will take Burke a few minutes to get the horses for you and will give us time to get acquainted?"

"I'd be delighted, Mr. Collier."

"You will join us, Sir Charles?"

"Delighted!"

The study was a small, quiet room off the hall. It was lined with books and had huge leather chairs—a man's room, furnished for comfort. "Please be seated, I'll have some coffee brought in."

When he had given the order, he came back and seated himself. "Now tell me about it. What happened to bring you West?"

"My father passed away at the beginning of the war and only a few months after my marriage to Major Breydon. The major was away with his command, and during and after the Battle of Bull Run, the plantation was virtually destroyed; our stock was driven off and the crops ruined.

"Major Breydon was wounded, lost an arm, in fact, and while he was still in the hospital, our plantation was raided by guerrillas. They stole the few of our horses that remained, burned Harlequin Oaks, and killed some of our people. Fortunately, I escaped."

"I am sorry. Sorry for the destruction but glad you escaped."

"The first part was the fortune of war, Mr. Collier. Our

plantation happened to be in the way. The second part, the raid by guerrillas, men who were simply thieves, was another thing entirely. These men were despised by soldiers of both the Union and the Confederacy, men who simply took advantage of a state of war to rob and kill. But there is no need to talk of that here."

The coffee was served with some small cakes. "It is good to see you again, Mary. You will never believe how much we, who were away from home, loved those long weekends at Harlequin Oaks. Not long ago, I was in Paris, and some of us who had been military attachés in Washington at the time were talking of those soirées at the plantation."

They talked then of riding to the hounds, of horses, and of people.

"And Major Breydon?" Sir Charles asked. "He is here now?"

"He was killed in Julesburg only a few months ago. He was shot down on the street."

"Oh, I'm sorry! Who could have done such a thing?"

"It was done," she replied quietly, "by the leader of the guerrillas. He saw himself recognized and shot my husband before he could be accused.

"My husband wore his gun in an army holster with a button-down flap. He was shot without warning, shot on sight."

There was a rap at the door; then it opened. "Mr. Collier? I was told I would find you here. I wish—"

It was Jason Flandrau.

"If you wish to know who would do such a thing," Mary Breydon said, "you might ask Mr. Flandrau."

Flandrau took in the situation at a glance. He had no idea what Mary Breydon was doing here, but that she was among friends was obvious. It was equally obvious that his plan to enlist the support of Preston Collier was no longer a possibility.

"I am sorry," he said. "I did not mean to interrupt."

He closed the door and stood for just an instant, shaking with fury. This was an end to it, then, all his work, all his planning, his great chance, all gone glimmering. There was but one thing to do now. He turned to the door and called for his horse.

"Do you mean to imply that Jason Flandrau was the leader of those guerrillas? But he came to me highly recommended! We have mutual friends!"

"I do not imply, Mr. Collier. I state it as a fact. You have been away, so perhaps you have not heard. An attempt was made to kill me only a few days ago. The attempt was made by a man referred to as Turkey Joe Longman. He was pursued, and in the gun battle that followed, he was killed. I believe he was one of the guerrillas.

"A few days before the attempt, Longman came to the stage station with a younger man whose name I do not know, but that younger man was riding a horse stolen from us and on which I still have the papers."

"But can you trace any of this to Flandrau?"

"I am afraid I cannot. The killing of my husband was ruled self-defense, as my husband was armed, and Jason Flandrau said my husband made a threatening gesture."

A man came to the door. "Sir? The team is ready, sir. Shall I accompany Mrs. Breydon?"

Mary stood up. "No, thank you. I shall be all right." She extended a hand to Preston Collier. "You have been most gracious."

Turning to Sir Charles, she said, "You have no idea what this means to me, to see someone from home. I had not realized I missed it so much! If you have a moment, please stop by the station. I can offer you nothing like this, but Matty is a wonderful cook, and the meals *are* good."

After she was gone, Preston Collier asked, "This Harlequin Oaks? It was a fine place?"

"There were people who preferred an invitation to Harlequin Oaks to any other place on the eastern seaboard. Claybourne had the finest horses and the best food a man could find and an excellent cellar with it. The home place was about four hundred acres of as fine land as I have seen, but they had more back in the mountains, some six hundred acres of timberland. I know it well, as we often went there to hunt.

"Once the war is over and the land can be brought back into production, she will be a very wealthy young woman."

"Odd that she would come West and take the kind of job she has."

"Not if you know the family. Very independent, very able. Her father was prepared to accept any responsibility, and after all, there is not much a young woman can do."

The wind blew cold along the Cherokee Trail, and raindrops blew from the leaves and spattered against her rain cape. It was a long ride back through the rain, yet she felt good, better than she had felt in days.

Seeing Sir Charles was only a part of it, as was the kindly reception from Preston Collier and the defeat of Flandrau. That, she believed, was complete and final as far as his political ambitions were concerned. Even had he planned otherwise, Collier was too wise a man to back the political aspirations of a man liable to such an accusation. The young, ambitious newspapers of Colorado would crucify anyone who supported such a man.

Yet it did not lessen her danger. If she were destroyed, he might still have a chance, although a slim one. Especially if she could be eliminated in such a way as not to implicate him.

Thinking about it coolly, Mary Breydon faced that fact. Her troubles were far from over, yet she doubted if another attempt would be made with firearms. Now he must be more subtle. Whatever was done must seem to be an accident.

It was long after midnight when at last she led the horses into the yard at Cherokee.

Wat opened the barn door. "Better bring 'em in here, ma'am."

"Wat! What are you doing up at this hour?"

"Me an' Ridge, we been takin' turns watchin' out for you. He just gotten himself to sleep. If'n we're quiet, he'll go right on sleepin'."

When the horses were stalled, she tiptoed inside and, sitting alone beside the fire, drank a cup of coffee from the blackened pot. It was very hot and very black, and it tasted good.

For a moment, after she was in bed, she lay awake looking up at the darkness where the ceiling was. She could not remember a time when she had gone to bed so pleased with herself and the situation.

The horses had been stolen, yet she had found others, and tomorrow the stage would leave on time.

Nobody could have done it better, not Temple Boone or even Mark Stacy.

She was smiling when she fell asleep.

SEVENTEEN

When the stage had gone and Peg had finished gathering the dishes from the tables, she looked over at Wat, who was looking at something in his hand.

"What's that?"

"Arrowhead."

"Can I see?"

He held it out on his open palm. "Where did you get it?"

He waved a hand toward the hill rising beyond the trees. "Yonder. There's an old Indian camp."

"Could I find one?"

"Maybe. If you look sharp and if you're lucky."

"Will you take me?"

"I don't know. What would your mother say?"

"She wouldn't mind. It isn't far, is it?"

"No, just over yonder. Just a few minutes. I don't know, though. You'd be scared."

"Scared? What is there to be scared of?"

"Ghosts. Ghosts of dead Indians. Some say they hang around old camps."

"Have you seen one? A ghost, I mean?"

"No, I never. That doesn't say they ain't none. I found a dead Indian once. I found his skull and some bones. Some ribs and the spine."

"What did you do?"

"I covered him up again. Pa said never to disturb the remains. He said it was all right to pick up arrowheads but not to disturb their graves. If they were very, very old, he said somebody should study them who understood what he was doing. Somebody who knew what he was seeing.

"He told me one time that he found a cut bank where a stream had washed away the bank, and there in plain sight were three camps, each one a few inches or a few feet above the other, and each one was different, different kind of arrowheads, like that."

He turned the arrowhead in his fingers, then handed it to Peg. "You can have that. Some Indian made it a long time ago. Come on, I'll show you where I found it."

She put the arrowhead in her pocket. "Thank you, Wat. That's the first thing a boy ever gave me."

"Aw, it ain't nothin'! You wait! I know where there's jasper and sometimes other kinds of stones. That ol' arrowhead ain't nothin'."

"It is so. I *like* it."

"Come on. I'll show you where I found it. It's just over yonder. We won't be gone very long."

"Shouldn't we tell mother?"

"It's just over there. You'll be back before she knows you're gone. Anyway, you don't have to be scared. I'll take care of you."

"I'm *not* scared!"

Walking together, they started away toward the hill beyond the nearest trees. There was a narrow draw there and a bare place in the midst of the brush and close to one side of the draw.

"See?" Wat indicated a circle of fire-blackened stones almost covered with dirt and sand. "That was where they built their fires. Now if we look around—"

"Did you come here looking for arrowheads?"

"Not really. The first time it was with pa. That was just after the stage station was built. Pa had his wagon, and we were fetching bones—"

"*Bones?*"

"We used to go out and pick up old bones, buffalo bones, antelope, anything like that. When pa got a wagonload he'd drive it into town and sell it."

"Sell *bones?* Who would want some smelly old bones?"

"They weren't smelly! They were *old*. They grind them up for fertilizer and some other stuff. I don't know what-all."

"People bones?"

"No, silly. Buffalo bones, most of them. There were some others. One time pa found a tusk, like from an elephant? Like you see in pictures? He told some people in Denver about it, but they wouldn't come to look. Said it was nonsense. Pa sold it to a peddler for twenty dollars."

"Twenty dollars? For an old bone?"

"It was a tusk. Ivory. Pa said it was probably worth more, but twenty dollars was a lot of money, and he didn't know of anybody who wanted it. Pa said he could eat good for two months on twenty dollars."

Wat stopped suddenly, picking up a piece of stone almost as large as a man's fist. It was chipped along one edge. "See this here? Indians chip off flakes of stone to make hide scrapers. After they skin a buffalo, they use these to scrape off the fat on the underside."

"Oh . . . look! I found an arrowhead!" She held it up for his inspection.

"You sure did!" Wat was pleased. Suddenly his expression changed. "Look! Look yonder!"

He pointed to a track just beyond where she had found the arrowhead. It was a boot track, a large boot track.

"What is it?" Peg was puzzled.

"Ssh!" He gestured for silence. "Look there! It's fresh!" His voice was low but intense. "That was made this mornin'!"

"How do you know?" Disbelief was obvious in her tone.

"Look," he said. "It rained some last night. Not much, but some. See how the ground is speckled by the big drops? And the wind blew, too.

"Well, there's no speckles in that track, and the edges are sharp and clear."

"Maybe Mr. Fenton was over here."

"Ridge? Naw, he won't take a step out of the area least he has to or there's a fight shapin' up. He makes like he's scared an' doesn't want to get into a fight, but you just try keepin' him out of one. That ol' codger would tackle a grizzly and give him first swat! No, siree! I know who made that track! It was Scant Luther!"

"Wat? Let's go home. I'm scared." Then she said, "How could you tell it's his track? It's just an old boot track!"

"I seen his tracks many's the time. See there? That patched place? He fixed that himself. And this place where the heel's run down? He walks like that. You watch him."

"I don't ever want to see him. Wat, let's go home."

"We can't. Least, I can't. I got to see what he's doin', and you can bet your hide he's up to no good. He hates your mama."

"What can we do?"

"Foller him a little ways. See where he's goin', then tell Ridge or Temple Boone."

Eagerly, he started casting about for tracks. "He's got a long stride, bein' big like he is. Stay behind me now."

"What difference does his stride make?"

"Tells you where to look for the next step. About two and a half feet, I'd guess." Wat looked around, then suddenly pointed. "There! In the sand alongside that rock. See? He stepped on the rock, but his foot slid off a mite and made that mark in the sand. Come on, but be very quiet! And don't talk!"

Wat moved swiftly. Scant Luther, not expecting to be trailed, had made no attempt to cover his tracks. He walked swiftly, taking long strides, and if occasionally he stepped on rocks, it was simply because it was easier.

Wat stopped suddenly, and putting his lips close to her ear, he whispered, "I smell smoke!"

He started on, then stopped and whispered again. "If you have to run, run uphill. The station's right over this ridge, and besides, you can run uphill faster'n he can. On the level, he'll catch you. Goin' uphill, he's too heavy!"

They started on, tiptoeing through the sand, slipping through the brush to make no sound. Peg was scared, but she was excited, too. This was fun! She had never done anything like this before. What would mama think? And Matty?

Suddenly, Wat lifted a hand. Too late! She was too close behind him, and he stopped so abruptly that she bumped into him, staggering him into a dry bush.

Scant Luther, crouching over his campfire, looked up, right into her eyes.

With a gruff roar, he lunged to his feet, staggering a little. Peg was off like a rabbit, running up the steep hill, dodging brush and rocks. Behind her, she could hear Scant's big boots scratching gravel, but she feared to look back.

Off on her left and a little ahead of her, Wat was scrambling up the same steep hillside. He was just passing a big rock—

He stopped abruptly and threw himself behind the rock. "Help me!" he yelled.

Scrambling, she got behind the rock. It moved, it tilted, and suddenly it began to roll, a slow, ponderous roll; then it fell free and started downhill, leaping and bounding, right at Scant Luther!

He heard it, looked up, eyes bulging. Then he gave a great leap to one side and hit the hillside rolling. Down he went, the boulder tumbling past him, missing by a hair's breadth.

Scant started to rise, staggered, and fell again.

"Quick!" Wat said. "The other one!"

Running after him, Peg threw herself behind a second, somewhat smaller rock. Down it went, leaping and bounding, followed by a torrent of small rocks, some of them leaping high in the air as they toppled and fell.

"Come on, let's run!" Scrambling, they went up the hill and, breathless, paused at the top, hand in hand, to look back.

From where they now stood, they could no longer see Scant Luther, only dust rising from the hillside.

"Let's go," Wat said. "I should never have brought you out here."

"Mama will be angry."

"We've got to tell her," Wat said. "She's got to know he's over there."

Matty came to the door to throw out some wash water just as they came into the yard. She stopped, looking at them.

"So it's trouble you've been makin'?"

"How did you know?" Peg asked.

"Sure it stands out all over the two of you! A blind man could see it. Now come here an' tell me. What is it you've done?"

As she spoke, Ridge Fenton came to the door, a piece of apple pie in his hand. As they explained, he began to grin. "By the Lord Harry, I'd of give a pretty piece to've seen that! Ol' Scant a scramblin' for his life!" He slapped his leg, his mouth stuffed with pie. When he could talk again, he said, "Too bad one o' those rocks didn't bust him on the head!"

Mary, preparing her supply list, listened, half in anger, half relief. Then she got up and came to the door. "Wat, first I want to thank you for getting Peg safely home, but don't you ever do that again! She is not to leave the yard without telling me. Do you understand? You both might have been killed by that awful man!"

"Yes'm," Wat said sheepishly. "I'm sorry, ma'am. It was only a little way, and I didn't reckon anybody was around."

"He's gone by now," Fenton said. "He knows we know, and he don't know but what Boone is around. Boone would go huntin' him, sure as shootin'."

"I don't want you to go, Ridge," Mary said. "We want you here."

"Now don't you worry yourself about that, ma'am. I just don't cotton to goin' off in the hills huntin' Scant Luther. If'n he brings trouble to us, I'll speak my piece, an' it'll be language he understands."

"We must all be careful," Mary said. "We do know he is around, and Wat? I want to thank you for discovering him."

"He's a good boy," Matty said when she came inside. "You cannot blame them, children as they are. It's only natural they should go pokin' about, and certainly I did it myself.

"We had no outlaws or Indians about, but we had high cliffs along the shore and the sea and the caves in the cliffs where sometimes we went when the tide was out.

"Lookin' back, I can see it was fearsome risks we took, climbin' about in those caves like we done. It was a wonder the sea never trapped us there, and there were times when we scarcely made it out before the caves flooded. But that's the way with youngsters, mum."

After they were all inside, she went to the door herself and stepped out in the almost dark and stood in the shadow of the station, looking westward.

That was where the mountains were, higher mountains than she had ever seen, as high as the Alps but more of them, they said. Someday she must go there. She must take Peg and Wat and go to the mountains, yet even here there was something in the air that was different. It was so clear, so different from what she had been used to.

She watched the first stars come out, and suddenly she wished Marshall were there, standing beside her, just to feel with her, to realize with her that she was changing, and she knew what the change portended. She no longer longed to return to the plantation. To rebuild Harlequin Oaks . . . yes. She must do that. She had promised herself that, promised that to the memory of her father and to Peg.

For herself, she knew now it would never be enough, for she had changed. She had become a western woman.

EIGHTEEN

J ason Flandrau's first instinct was to run, yet he had built too
well here, and he had no desire to return to the old days of
riding and hiding. Returning to Denver, he studied all aspects
of his situation.

After all, it was one woman's accusation. Admittedly, he
must forget any assistance from Preston Collier, for the latter
would not risk his position and prestige backing a candidate
whose reputation was tainted. All right, then, Collier must be
forgotten. Who were Collier's rivals? Who were his enemies?

Flandrau had already discovered that people were reluctant
to think evil of anyone who dressed and talked well and who
maintained an outward appearance of respectability. He had a
good singing voice, and like almost every boy of his time, he
had gone to church regularly, if only to meet the girls, and he
knew most of the hymns.

So he would continue on the course he had set for himself,
careful to keep himself to respectable circles. He must develop
a mine or ranch where he could hire men and so have contact
with those he needed without arousing unwelcome curiosity.

Mary Breydon must, of course, be eliminated, but now it

135

must be done by accident or by Indians. Traveling was rough, the horses often only half broken. There were many things that could happen, only he must make sure that one of them happened to her.

Scant Luther? If he acted against her, nobody would be surprised, and it would not be linked to Flandrau.

Scant . . . Indians . . . accident.

One or the other should provide an answer, and whatever accusations she made would quickly be forgotten. Now he must think, he must plan—

Of course, there was Denver Cross, but Cross he wished to keep out of sight and out of trouble until he, Flandrau, became governor. Cross was no fool and too valuable a man to be wasted. He would be needed later.

Scant first . . . Cross could handle that or, better still, Jordy Neff. Jordy, as Flandrau had been quick to recognize, had a mean streak. He liked to prod about until he found something about which a man was sensitive and then work on it. It was a form of sadistic torture at which Neff was adept.

A few days later, pausing on the street near Neff but without seeming to notice him, Flandrau said, "See anything of Scant? I wonder how he likes being made a fool of by that woman?"

Neff chuckled. "He don't like it much. He's been muttering in his beard, making threats."

"He could save us a lot of trouble, Neff. Prod him a little."

Flandrau walked on up the street. There was that little ranch up the river. Maybe he could make a deal for it, a quiet place, out of sight, easily reached, and with trails heading back into the mountains.

His every instinct warned him that now was the time to leave. There were other places, other times. Yet there was in him a streak of stubbornness, a refusal to be defeated by a woman and the realization that he might never again find such a situation as he had come upon here.

He was not sanctimonious. He was simply quietly respectful. On several occasions, he had been asked to sing solos and had done so. He was not a great singer but had come from a family where there was much singing, and he had grown up around camp meetings and revivals, so all the hymns, the prayers, the quotations, came easily to him.

He was a man who believed in nothing, a man totally selfish, totally self-centered, completely ruthless. To be defeated by a mere woman was absurd. Preston Collier would have been useful, but he was not necessary. He would have Mrs. Breydon eliminated and would press on. So far, his name had not appeared in the newspapers, and he wanted it that way. If he could begin by winning a large number of voters, right at the grass roots, when his name was finally brought forward, he would have easy sailing. Carefully, he began considering his next move.

What was needed was a good rain. Not a piddling few drops but a rain, something to settle the dust, for at Cherokee dust was the enemy and the cause of much of the work that must be done. Every stage and every rider-by started up a cloud of dust, and it settled on everything.

Matty was alone, and she was baking. She loved baking and especially she liked making cookies, pies, and doughnuts. Doughnuts were new to her, for she had never seen one until she came to this land, but she liked making them and liked seeing them eaten. Coming from a large family of healthy boys, she knew what an appetite was. Or she thought she did.

Then there was the day when the Indians came.

Mary Breydon had taken Peg and gone off to Laporte to pick up some things needed about the place. Ridge Fenton had gone hunting.

At breakfast, he had said, "I'm hungerin' for wild meat. I'm goin' to fetch some. Antelope, maybe, although I don't cotton to antelope. Too stringy, gets in my teeth. Buffler, that's what I want. Come right down to it, I'd rather have a nice fresh lion. Mountain lion. Cougar. Ain't no better meat anywhere than cougar meat."

He glanced across the table at Peg. "You got to kill 'em first. They're too lively to eat right off the hoof."

"Cougars don't have hoofs!" Peg said. "They have paws."

" 'Course they do! Maws, too. I'm that hungry for wild meat

I could eat paw, maw, and the kittens. The whole batch." He pushed back from the table and wiped his mustache with the back of his hand. "You just set by. I'll take ol' Betsy out there an' run down a buffler, a deer, somethin' of the kind. Maybe I can back an ol' grizzly into a corner."

"A *grizzly?*" Wat stared at him. "Nobody in his right mind wants to corner a *grizzly!*"

"Hate to do it," Ridge explained. "Really hate to do it! Them grizzlies, they *know* me. Once they see me comin', they know the end is near. Why some of them back up an' cry! They just cry like babies because they know when they see ol' Ridge a-comin' totin' ol' Betsy that their time has come.

"They know their days of free roamin' is over and they are about to become steaks an' mince meat. Ever eat a mince meat pie made from fresh grizzly? Ain't nothin' better.

"All summer long, that grizzly has been fattenin' up on nuts, berries, roots, and the like, mixed in with a fresh young buffler, maybe a papoose or two, so he's *ready!* I mean he's fat.

"Of course, I never kill a grizzly lest he's fat. Sometimes, when they are runnin' to get away, I have to run up beside them and pinch their ribs to see if they're fat enough. When I pinch 'em, they know why, an' they screech like banshees because they know what's comin', an' they are sorry for all those berries and nuts they been eatin'. Right then, they wished it was less."

"Don't pay any attention, Peg," Wat said. "He's just yarnin'."

Ridge glared. "Yarnin', is it? You just wait. One o' these days, I'll take you a-huntin' with me, an' you can pinch 'em for fat your own self! You'll see what I mean."

He rested his hands on his knees, staring at them. "Ever eat beaver tail? Now that's mighty fine eatin'! Next to cougar, there's nothin' like beaver tail or buffler tongue. Finest meat anywhere!"

Ridge Fenton had been gone for more than an hour when the Indians came. She caught a movement from the corner of her eye and went to the window. There could have been no less than thirty of them, possibly more. At least eight men, ten or twelve women, and some children. They were mounted and pulling travoises piled with their tepees and goods.

Matty was appalled. Since coming to Cherokee, she had heard a dozen stories of how Indians could eat. Three of them had been known to eat a buffalo at a sitting, and those Indians out there—why there'd be nothing left for the stage! What to do?

They had stopped out by the corral now, and two of them were approaching the station. Matty took up the shotgun and put it beside the door.

"They respect courage," somebody had said, "and not much else." Well, maybe. Matty did not know; all she had was courage. Suddenly, before they reached the step, she jerked open the door.

The action was so sudden the Indians stopped, startled. "What do you want?" she demanded. She had the shotgun by the door but a broom in her hands.

"Eat," one of the Indians said. He was a broad, strong-looking man with his hair in two braids. "We hungry."

"Go hunt, then," Matty said. "Go find a fat grizzly. Feel of his ribs to see if he's fat enough first."

They stared at her. Straight-faced, hiding the fact that she was frightened, she remembered what Ridge Fenton had been telling the children. "If he's not fat enough, let him go."

One of the Indians scowled and muttered something to the other, who began to explain. They both turned to look at Matty, who looked right back at them.

"We hungry," an Indian repeated.

"Find a fat bear or a buffalo." She looked beyond the men at the Indian children. Their eyes were wide and dark, their faces round and serious.

"I won't feed you," she said, "but I'll feed the little ones. The papooses," she said, remembering the word from Ridge Fenton and hoping it was the right one. "Not you or you," she pointed at them. "You can hunt for meat. Send me the little ones, the papooses."

The two Indians returned to the cavalcade and there was much talk, and then slowly the children began getting down from the horses and hesitantly approached.

There were nine of them. One larger boy, evidently already

a man in his own mind, would not come but stood back, disdainfully proud.

Seating them at an outside table, she filled a bowl of stew for each of them. She would have to cook again, but no matter.

She stood over them while they ate, slowly, solemnly, often looking up at her. The men stayed by their horses, watching. Finally, when they were eating the last of their stew, she told them to wait. Going inside, she covered a tray with cookies and took them outside.

The children stared at her, then at the cookies. She held up one finger, looking very stern. "One!" she said. "No more!"

Then she passed the cookies. Solemnly, still without smiling, each one took a cookie, looking up at her to be sure they were doing the right thing but looking hungrily at the rest of the cookies on the tray.

Suddenly, Matty turned and walked out to the waiting Indians and passed the cookies to the men and then the women. Very carefully, each Indian took just one. When the tray was empty but for one cookie, she looked at it, then at them. Then she took up the last cookie and ate it herself. One of the Indians started to chuckle and muttered something to the others, and they all laughed.

The young ones scrambled back on their ponies or the travoies, and slowly the little cavalcade moved away. As they moved off, she lifted a hand and waved. After a moment, one of the children waved back.

Matty went inside and closed the door. Suddenly, she dropped to a bench, heaving a great sigh. She'd been scared, and she was still scared.

After a moment, she got up. "An' just for that," she said aloud, "I'll spend me mornin' cookin'!"

Hours later, Ridge Fenton came down the road, and when he saw the tracks, he stopped, stared at them, then broke into a run. When he was almost at the station, Matty stepped out, hands on her hips.

"What is the matter, then? Is it frightened you are? Come in, then, an' be safe."

"What happened?" Ridge demanded. "Woman, what happened?"

"Nothing, nothing at all! Some Indians came by, we talked, and they went on."

He stared at her. "What happened? Don't tell me you got by without feedin' that lot?"

"They all were very nice," she said, "and they had better manners than some others I know." She paused. "I just told them when I wanted fat meat, I pinched grizzlies until I found one fat enough."

"You're funnin' me." He stared at her. "Now see here, woman, I—!"

"Go do your chores," she said. "You're late."

Four days later, Mary Breydon was sweeping the doorstep when she saw two Indians riding up. One of them had what was obviously a haunch of fresh venison tied up in the deer's hide.

They reined up at the door. "Where is Woman-Who-Pinches-Bears?" one Indian demanded.

Hearing them, Matty came to the door.

"Where papooses?" one Indian asked solemnly.

Matty turned. "Peg? Wat?"

When they came to the door, the Indian very solemnly handed the fresh meat to Wat. Then he glared at Matty. "No for you! Papooses!"

Then they rode away, but as they reached the place where the road turned, they looked back. Matty waved, and they waved in return.

NINETEEN

There were no days without work, but now the work had fallen into patterns, and each knew what must be done.

"That Wat," Ridge Fenton said one morning, "if he keeps on the way he's goin', he'll work me out of a job!"

"The lad's no blacksmith," Matty said, "although he's good with horses."

"No blacksmith, is it? He watches me all the time, helps when he can. That boy's learnin' too durned fast!"

Later, Matty asked Wat, "Is it a smith you're goin' to be? Mr. Fenton says you are pickin' it up an' rarely fast."

"No, ma'am. I don't figure to be no blacksmith, but every man should have him a trade, something to fall back on in time of need."

"What do you really want to be?" Mary asked.

Wat flushed and looked down at his plate. "I'd like to write stories like that Sir Walter Scott you read from."

"It's hard work, Wat, and very few writers make a good living."

"That Sir Walter Scott did. Temple Boone said he did mighty well."

"Temple Boone told you that?" She was surprised.

"It's true, ain't it?"

"Yes, it is. He was a very popular writer. So were Charles Dickens and William Shakespeare. They all did very well."

She paused. "How did Mr. Boone happen to tell you that?"

"He was readin' him. He was reading a book by Sir Walter Scott. He was slow at it, he said, but he was going to get better and read faster. He said a man could be anything he wants to be if he'll just try hard enough."

"And what does Mr. Boone want to be?"

Wat looked at her slyly. "He'll most likely tell you hisself when he gets around to it."

She exchanged a look with Matty. "We can all improve ourselves, Wat. In these days, with books so easily had, there's no reason for anyone not to have an education. And if you want to be a writer, you should be reading a lot and not just the sort of thing you wish to write but other things as well."

After Wat had returned to the stable, Matty said, "He's a fine upstanding man, mum. Mr. Boone is a man any girl might set her cap for."

"It is too soon for me to think of that, Matty. I was very much in love with Marshall, and he's never far from my thoughts. Anyway, I must go back to Virginia when the war is over. After all, my home is there, and Peg's future."

"I've been wonderin' about that, mum. You gettin' more western all the time. You've changed, mum, whether you recognize it or not."

"Maybe."

"And there's that nice Mr. Stacy. He's a good man, too, with a good job, and he's one who will do well. Folks talk of buildin' a railroad west after the war, and they say he's mixed up with it somehow."

She straightened up from the washboard where she had been washing clothes. "What I like about this country is that nobody thinks anything is too big or too hard. If they want to do something, they just take it for granted they can do it, and then they just naturally go ahead."

She scrubbed for a few minutes and then said, "Although Mr. Boone says, and I think he's right, that the railroads will change the country for the worse. They'll make it richer, but the people will be different.

"Now it takes them a while to get here, and they hear a lot of talk and pick up a certain way of thinking. Western folks have standards. They have a certain way of behaving toward women and toward each other, and when they make a deal, their word is enough.

"When the railroads get in, Mr. Boone thinks that will change. A lot of people will be coming West with different ways and ideas. He may be right. I met some people back East I wouldn't want to see out here."

"But all of us came from back East!"

"Yes, mum, we did, but the West has a way of weeding out the bad ones, or they don't last. There's a few, like Scant Luther, but mighty few.

"That outlaw Johnny Havalik, the one who gave his boots to Wat, they say he'd never rob a woman. He'd stop a stage and take the money from everybody else but never from a woman."

When she had finished ironing and folding the clothes, Mary Breydon walked outside. There was a feeling of change in the air, the first touch of spring, probably, although it was a bit early for that.

She stood looking down the valley. How quickly one forgot! She could hardly believe there was a war on and that people whom she knew were fighting and dying. It all seemed so far from here, as though it were another world, yet there was a difference, and it was not only in the air.

Everybody who came West was coming to build, some to build in the West, some merely to get rich and get out, but all were intending to do great things, to grow, to achieve. She heard the talk of the stage passengers while they were eating. None of them seemed to have any doubts; none of them seemed worried by Indians, by deserts, mountains, or the wilderness.

This was their land of Canaan, the land where dreams came true, but here there was a difference, for each one of them seemed sure that he had to make the dreams come true, that it would be the result of something he *did*.

Peg came out and stood beside her. "It's nice, isn't it, mama?"

"Yes, it is, Peg."

How long before the war was over? How long before they could think of returning? And what about Peg? Her memories would be of Cherokee Station, and when she looked back, it would be at these quiet hills, at these weather-worn buildings, at memories of Matty, Wat, and Mr. Boone.

Peg had been too young. She could scarcely be expected to remember the parties, the balls, the beautifully dressed people, the music and the house with its white columns and its vine-covered walls. She would have no memories of the smartly trotting horses bringing the black, varnished carriages to their door and the people getting down from them and her father welcoming them at the door.

All in the past, and they were *her* memories, not Peg's.

"Matty?" The Irish girl had come to the door to throw out some water. "We must find that land, file claims for ourselves. When the war is over, there will be thousands of people coming West, all wanting land."

"Yes, mum, I'd like a bit of land, a place with trees and a stream."

"Maybe we should look further west? In the mountains?"

"It's like the rest of them, mum. No matter where you are, there is always something else that might be better, just a little further west."

It was true, of course. Wandering got into the blood, and there were always those greener pastures that lay over the fence or over the next range of mountains.

Here all was strange and new yet somehow familiar. Western men and women had little time for contemplation, although Temple Boone said he did most of his thinking alongside a campfire or when riding. Western men were thinking of how things could be done; they were used to making do. Since coming to Cherokee, she had heard several stories of men alone who had set their own broken bones, amputated limbs, doing what could be done to survive. Only a few miles away, two sisters had built their own log cabin.

Yet she was hungry for news from home. There were few

letters, but newspapers were occasionally left at the station, and a couple of men had left books. She listened hungrily to the talk among the passengers. So much was happening in the world, and she heard so little of it.

Back home, there would be talk, much of it idle chatter, of course, but there would be talk of government and policy, of art, music, and books, of what was happening in Europe and occasionally even in Asia or Africa.

Henry Wadsworth Longfellow had just published *Tales of a Wayside Inn,* Jules Verne had written *Five Weeks in a Balloon,* and George Eliot had published *Romola.* In Paris, Bizet had a new opera, *Les Pescheurs,* and people back East and even out here were singing "When Johnny Comes Marching Home" and "Clementine." A man in New York had invented something they called roller skates that had little rubber wheels instead of blades. A French firm had begun selling Perrier water bottled at a spring near Nîmes.

An American writer, Nathaniel Hawthorne, had died, and so had the French artist Delacroix. U.S. Grant had been made commander in chief of the Union armies. Mary had never heard of him until some victories were won in the West. He had never been considered among the great generals, like Meade or McClellan. Someone on one of the stages had said that he and Lee had served together in the war with Mexico.

"We're so far from everything!" she spoke suddenly, impatiently. "We're missing so much, Matty!"

"Yes, mum, but look about you. We are where so much is happening and where so much is about to happen. I think we are fortunate, mum, because we are among the first. If we look about us, I think we can both become rich women, and I do not mean by simply marrying some man who has it."

She gestured westward. "They are finding gold and silver in the mountains, mum. There was a man stopped by the other mornin', a man with a horse and two donkeys, and he was headed west, worried about food supplies and blastin' powder, mum."

She twisted the water from a towel. "I grubstaked him, mum."

"You did *what?*"

"When you put up the money for a prospector's supplies, they call it 'grubstakin',' and if he makes a strike, a find of gold or silver, that is, then you share in it."

"How much of a share?"

"One-third, mum." She dried her hands and took from her pocket a paper. "He signed this, mum. If he makes a find, I get one-third of it all, forever."

"What if you never see him again?"

"I'll hear it if he finds anything, and if he does na come to me with it, I will surely go to him. He's an Irishman, mum, and although the Good Lord knows there are thieves among us, too, I told him I'd go to Cork and look up his kinfolk there and tell them what a blackguard he'd become. I'd also set the law on him." She smiled a little. "Or maybe Ridge Fenton or Temple Boone."

"How much did you give him?"

"All I'd saved, mum, but I shall eat here, and there will be a bit of a wage comin' to me soon, and I'm going nowhere at all."

She took up her tub to carry to the door. "Here he comes, mum. Temple Boone, I mean, and you'd better fix your hair a mite."

Mary gave her an exasperated look. "I shall fix my hair, and thank you for telling me, but I am not, as you phrased it, 'settin' my cap' for Temple Boone!"

"You could do worse, mum. He's a bit on the rough and wild side, but a true man, with it all, and mum, they are hard to come by!"

A quick look in the mirror did show a strand of loose hair here and there. She straightened it with quick, deft fingers. She was not interested in Temple Boone, but nonetheless—

He paused inside the door, hat in hand, giving her a quick, approving glance, and she was glad she had straightened her hair. "Mind if I pour myself some coffee, Mrs. Breydon? No reason for me to disturb you, I'm just sort of passin' through."

"Do help yourself, Mr. Boone. Did Matty tell you that the children almost ran upon Scant Luther?"

"He's been scoutin' around, ma'am. It's about time I gave him his walkin' papers."

"There's no need. I still have my pistol."

He smiled. "Havin' a pistol and knowin' when to use it are two different things. Use your best judgment, ma'am, but don't wait too long. Luther has no business here, and the company does not want him around. If he comes, it is because he is fixin' to cause trouble. And don't waste time reasonin' with him. He knows what the game is. Tell him to get off, and if he makes a step toward you, shoot him. It isn't as if he was a stranger. You know him and what he's like."

Boone sat down with his coffee. "There's talk around, ma'am. Your station is makin' a name for itself, and it is being talked of as an overnight station."

"But we haven't room!"

"That's just it. They'd build on some sleepin' rooms. Add to the place." He sipped his coffee. "Mean something to you, too, ma'am, because your salary would go up."

She had not thought of that. It would not be much, of course, but it would help.

"I suppose I must thank Mark Stacy for that."

"No, ma'am. You did it yourself, you and Matty and the others. Whenever you offer good food, good service, and a bright, friendly atmosphere, you will be talked about. Travelers tell each other, and about the bad places, too."

He refilled his cup, straddling the bench beside the table. "I've been thinkin', ma'am. I mean I've been thinkin' about you. Now—"

"Mum? That man Jordy Neff? He's comin' down the road, and he's ridin' with two others."

Temple Boone turned sharply to look up the road. Then he reached back and slipped the loop from the hammer of his six-shooter.

"I see him." Mary Breydon's expression changed. "And he's riding my horse!"

TWENTY

Temple Boone watched Jordy Neff dismount. His features were tight and hard. "Mrs. Breydon," even the tone of his voice had changed, "are you ready for trouble?"

"What kind of trouble?"

"Shooting trouble," he replied.

"The stage is coming in," she said. "Nothing can happen until it is gone."

"Tell that to Neff," he said. "His kind doesn't wait, and that's Williams and Mody Mercer with him." He turned to look at her. "This is killing trouble. Where's Peg?"

"She's across the road, in our house. When the stage comes in, she will come over to help."

"She mustn't. She's got to stay there." As Mary started to move, he put up a hand. "No! Stay here! She will have to take her chances."

"What do you mean? Why should there be trouble?"

"Flandrau's been wanting to be rid of you. Jordy is his pet killer, and as for Mercer, he'll stop at nothing, just nothing at all."

"But the stage—!"

149

Boone turned to Matty. "Serve them, serve the stage people, too."

Mary Breydon stood staring out of the window. "That horse is mine!" Suddenly she was angry. "If they want trouble, they can have it!"

"Mary! Mrs. Breydon, think what you're doing. The men you're lookin' at are utterly vicious. You've never seen their like!"

"Oh, yes, I have! They raided Harlequin Oaks! They killed some of our people! They ran off our stock!"

He stared at her. Didn't she realize there were three of them, and it was he alone against them?

Where was Ridge Fenton? Where the hell was Ridge?

He could take—maybe he could take Neff, but what about the others?

"Mrs. Breydon." He spoke softly. "For God's sake, don't say anything about that horse! Not now!"

"I'll do no such—!"

"Here comes the stage," Matty said. She wiped her hands on her apron, smoothed down her dress. "Ma'am? The stage is here."

It came around the corner at a spanking trot, swung around the half circle, and pulled up at the station. Jordy Neff and his men were just outside the door. They turned to look.

"Matty?" Boone whispered. "Where's the shotgun?"

She gestured toward the bedroom door. "Right inside my door, left-hand side."

He backed up toward the door, his cup of coffee in his left hand. Jordy first . . . he would be the quickest one, then Mercer and Williams—

He was good with a gun, and he knew he was good, but *three* of them?

And a perfect chance for Mary Breydon to be killed, accidentally. An innocent bystander.

They swung open the door and came in, just ahead of the passengers. Neff stared across the table at Boone. "Well, what d'you know? Temple Boone! Look what we got here, fellas, Temple Boone!"

He stared at Boone, smiling a little. "You killed Longman, didn't you? He was a friend of mine."

"He was a thief. He had it coming."

Neff laughed. "Of course, he did! He killed his share, Lord knows! Men, women, maybe children, I don't know, but I set store by him. We rode together."

The passengers were trooping in. There were nine of them, at least four of them with the mark of the West on them. Two were strong-looking men wearing gun belts. Two others were business types, but both were armed. All four were tanned and rugged.

Matty moved quickly, quietly, serving them the steaks she had prepared. They were elk meat and very good.

One of the newcomers glanced from Neff to Boone, then apparently nudged his companion. The man edged over, out of the line of fire.

Neff forked a piece of the steak into his mouth, and Mary Breydon said, "Mr. Neff, you are riding a stolen horse!"

His mouth was full; he was chewing, and he had another piece of meat on his fork, halfway to his mouth. Caught in midmovement, he stared; an ugly glint came into his eyes and passed.

He put down his fork slowly, chewed and swallowed. "Ma'am, you bein' a woman—"

"Mr. Neff, I said you are riding a stolen horse. The horse belongs to me. He was stolen in a guerrilla raid on my plantation at Harlequin Oaks."

Neff's face was a shade more pale. He glanced briefly at the men across from him. "There's a lot of horses, ma'am. It's easy to make a mistake, y' know. I—"

"This is no mistake, Mr. Neff. That horse was stolen, and he belongs to me." She reached into her pocket. "I had been planning to put these papers in the hands of the sheriff, but as long as you have brought the horse here, there may be no need of that.

"These papers," she added, "are the pedigree papers for the horse you have been riding. The horse belongs to me!"

Jordy Neff's face slowly began to flush. All eyes were on him. Who did this woman think she was, anyway? Callin' him like this in front of everybody? "You're makin' a mistake, lady," he said. "That there horse is mine."

"Sir?" She spoke to one of the men at the table. "I dislike to disturb your lunch, but would you step out there and look under that horse's mane? Look high up and you will find a C branded there."

"My father's name and mine before I was married was Claybourne. That horse was raised on Harlequin Oaks. She was a pet of mine."

"Ma'am? Are you accusin' me?"

"I am not. I am simply saying you are riding a horse that was stolen from me and for which I have the papers. Do you have a bill of sale, Mr. Neff?"

His face flushed a deeper red. He was fairly trapped and had no idea what to do. If he drew a gun here, somebody was going to get killed, and he had a feeling that maybe these strangers might take a hand.

Mody and Williams were there, but—

Williams slowly, carefully pushed back his corner of the bench and stood up. "I am going to pay you, ma'am. Is it two bits?"

He spoke carefully to be sure they heard him before he started to put his hand in his pocket. He took out some coins, placed the proper coin on the table, and took a slow step back, then walked quietly toward the door, followed by Mercer, who also paid.

The man came in from outside. "The C is there, ma'am. Looks to me like the horse is yours."

"I have the papers here," she said, "and the description of the horse."

Horse stealing was a hanging offense. There was a stage driver and a hostler out there; there were several men in here—he could almost feel the rope.

"Sorry, ma'am. I didn't know the horse was stole. Can I ride him back to town?"

"No, you cannot. The horse will remain here. If you will remove your saddle and bridle, please? You may ride the stage into town." She paused. "If you have the fare."

Neff's eyes were ugly. "If you were a man—!"

"I'm a man," Boone suggested mildly.

"Not in here!" Matty had the shotgun. "Outside with you all! *Now!*"

They moved outside, and some of the passengers began to board the stage.

Mercer and Williams stood to one side, about ten feet apart, facing the stage station.

Neff walked toward the barn, then turned sharply around, waiting.

Boone was at the door, but before he could stop her, Mary was past him. "Gentlemen? Will you board, please?

"Wilbur? When the passengers are aboard, will you take the stage out, please? At once?" She turned. "Mr. Neff? Unless you wish to walk, I'd suggest you get your gear and get aboard."

"I got business here," he said, watching the door.

Temple Boone spoke quietly from within the door. "Ma'am? Don't you *see?* It's you they want to kill."

For an instant, she stood still. Of course, how could she have been such a fool? Yet how could she now get inside? If she made such a move, would they not kill her at once? The stage started to move.

"Take them out, Wilbur!" she said. "Now!"

The stage rolled; dust arose and settled. They could hear it rattling off down the road, the sound slowly receding.

She stood alone in the bare trail before the stage station, and there were three men whose intention it was that she die.

She stood very still, head held high, trying to think of a way out. What should she do now?

Walk to the door? Walk toward them? Softly, the voice from the doorway said, "When I step out, you hit the dirt. Hit it hard, ma'am. It will be your only chance!"

Matty moved to a window. "Mr. Boone, I have the shotgun. I will take Mr. Williams."

Boone waited, running his tongue over his lips. From where he stood, he could not see Jordy Neff, but he knew where he stood. The advantage was Neff's. The instant Boone's body showed, Neff would fire.

All right, he told himself. *You may have to take one, but kill him! Don't leave these women alone with him. Whatever happens, kill him!*

Another voice suddenly came from the barn. "All right, Matty, you take Williams. I got Mercer. I got him right in the sights o' this ol' buffler gun!"

At that moment, another voice, a strange voice, broke in. "We three. We kill."

Three rifle barrels appeared from the corral bars.

Jordy Neff, poised to go for his gun, held his hand. Beads of sweat broke out on his brow. Slowly, very carefully, he lowered his hand. "Get your horse, Mercer," he said after a moment. "You've got the biggest horse. I'll have to double up with you."

Mercer crossed the yard, untied both horses, and led them out into the road. Williams mounted up, his features showing the shock.

Mercer hesitated, then mounted, and then Jordy Neff swung up behind him. The horse sidestepped at the unusual load, obviously unhappy with it, but they started off.

Neff turned. "I'll be around, Boone! You can expect me!"

When they were gone, Mary walked into the house and sat down. "Thank you, Mr. Boone. Thank you, very much!"

Matty went to the door, shading her eyes. "Who were the others?" she demanded. "Who—?"

Three Indians rode out from behind the corral, drawing up at the door.

"You? Oh, thank you!"

Their faces were solemn. "Not for you," one said. "For the papooses!"

And they rode away, laughing.

TWENTY-ONE

"**I** d'clare, woman," Ridge Fenton said, "livin' around you is like livin' next to a battleground. I'm an old man, ma'am. I ain't up to all this excitement. I figured I was in for a quiet, peaceful time when I come here. I aimed to settle down, calm my nerves, kind of ease into old age, sort of."

"Thank you, Mr. Fenton. When I heard your voice, I knew one man would be taken out of the fight."

"Mebbe. I don't miss very often. Not at that range and with a buffalo gun. I'd have cut him loose from his pockets, b'lieve me."

"It isn't over," Boone said. "I think I should ride into town. It's me an' Jordy Neff now."

"Please . . . leave him alone."

Temple Boone turned toward Mary. "I do not have much choice, ma'am. This is my country. I live here. I shall always live here. I do not want trouble, but there are some kinds of trouble that cannot be avoided.

"From now on, wherever I go, there is a chance he will be there, waiting. It is better to get it over with, once and for all."

"Makes sense, ma'am. Of course, 'twas me, now, I'd set up

155

on a ridge somewhere and wait for him. He opened the ball, ma'am. He stated it clear that he meant to kill Boone, so as far as Boone is concerned, it's open season on Neff. He laid it down, implied he'd shoot on sight, and when you do that, all the rules are off. You shoot 'em whenever an' however you can. On'y Boone won't do that. He'll go down there to face him fair an' square. That's a good way to get hisself kilt."

Stages came, and stages left. It was an endless round of meals, stages, passengers of all sorts and kinds. Actors, prospectors, gamblers, miners, hunters, newspapermen, homemakers and shady ladies, whiskey peddlers and weapons' salesmen, Indian agents, drummers, men and women from all over the world, of every sort and nationality.

The work fell into patterns that made it easier, though never easy. In a time and place when women were scarce, they averaged a proposal every three days, the proposals coming from old men and young men, from established mining, ranching, or business men, from drifting cowhands, prospectors, and every variety of male creature afloat.

"An' some of them mean it," Matty said, "but there be some who are only talkin' an' would be frightened to their death if you said 'yes' to them! But 'tis a lonely time for folks out here and no pleasure in returnin' to an empty house to hear naught but the echo of your own voice!

"Here, with us, 'tis different, for we're a family-like, and we've each other to share with. A family is a place where a body can share the no-account things, can talk of the little matters important only to ourselves, where we can laugh and cry and tell of the day-by-day happenings and then forget them." Matty took off her apron. "So now I'll be settin' by with a warm cup for myself and to chat a bit."

Mary Breydon went outside, standing for a moment in the warm sunlight. Suddenly, all this was very familiar, very real.

Was it here, then, that she would make her home? Was Virginia no longer to be a part of her life? Here she was doing something important. She was a part of the westward movement. In her own small way, she was helping to build America, helping to make so many dreams come true.

Before the war, she knew of this only as a vague place called the West. It was where people went and where so few returned. The East she knew was a place of established families, businesses that had been in operation for many years, children whose great-grandparents had been young together, and it had been a good world in so many ways, a safe world.

That was not true here. Everything was new; everything was building. It was rough, hard, and unpolished. The law was around but never in the way. Men were expected to handle their own difficulties, and courage was the most respected virtue, with integrity a close second. Many a man whom you might call a thief with impunity would shoot you if you called him a liar or a coward.

Temple Boone came outside and stood beside her. "It's a good country," he said. "Don't be judging it too harshly. We're young yet. We're still growin' up. Where society doesn't have the organization to handle trouble, we have to handle it for ourselves."

"I know." She watched the road. The stage would be coming soon. She smiled to herself as the thought came. Was her life to be governed now by arrivals and departures?

"I understand," she said to Boone, "that you are an admirer of Sir Walter Scott?"

He glanced at her. "I have read him, although I read badly. The people he writes of are much like us, I think, in temperament and war. My first ancestor in this country was a rebel transported from England to Barbados. I know too little of my family but tradition. That much I've been told, and even the name of the vessel. It was the *John Friggat* of Bristol."

He glanced up the road. "Yes, I like Scott. He speaks to us, I think, and in the Carolinas where I once lived and in Georgia, he is very popular."

"We will be reading from him tonight if you care to stay. I've been reading to Wat and to Peg nearly every night."

"I shall be there if all goes well." He touched his hat. "Now I have other business."

"Mother?" Peg took her hand, watching him walk away. "Do you like him?"

"He is a good man, I think."

"But do you *like* him?"

Mary smiled. "Don't be so persistent! I am not ready to think of that yet. Your father is still too close to me, and when I think of a man, I think of him. When I remember the good things, he was always a part of them. I want to keep those memories, for they were the richest and most beautiful part of my life.

"Besides, I have much to do! I have to keep this station and make it better. I have to find a school for you and Wat and make our home better than it is. I can do this myself."

"I think you like Mr. Stacy."

She laughed. "Are you trying to find a romance for me? Mark Stacy is a good man, too, I think. He's a successful man, and I believe he is a man who will go far.

"You want to remember, Peg, just romance is not enough. You may often imagine yourself in love, but always remember you have to *live* with that person from day to day, in sickness and in health, as they say.

"You will want to be proud of him when you introduce him to your friends, and you want him to be comfortable with them, as you must be with his friends. One must never marry a man thinking he will change or that you will change him. If he does or you do, then he will not be the same man you married, and the less for it.

"But this is no time to think of that! And I am not even sure I know what I am talking about. Go help Matty set the table for the stage!"

Where was Wat?

She walked across to the stable and looked inside. "Wat?" There was no answer.

The door of the tack room stood open. His bed was neatly made, but there was no sign of him.

Stepping outside, she glanced around. Ridge Fenton was sewing a piece of leather.

"Mr. Fenton? Have you seen Wat?"

"No, ma'am, not in some time. He's around somewhere. You looked in the barn?"

"He's not there."

"Come to think about it, he did say something about huntin' arrowheads. Said he was all caught up on his work, and he wanted to find somethin' special for Peg."

Of course! She should have thought of that; still it was not a place she wanted him to go. It was close enough, yet out of sight of the station.

What was she thinking about? The boy had run free as a wild animal before he joined them. He was a tough little fellow and knew more about getting along in the wilderness than she did. Perhaps more than any of them, Ridge included.

Still, she was going to read a little later, and she had not told him.

She turned up the narrow path into the trees. It was only a little way. She'd have to hurry because Temple Boone would be coming back soon.

It was very quiet. Once around the corner of the hill, if you could call it a corner, all sound of the station seemed to be cut off.

She went down through the trees. It was an open place, right down there—

There was a cry from the brush. "Ma'am! Go back! *Run!*"

She stepped through the trees, and Scant Luther was standing there, feet apart, grinning at her. Nearby, tied in a bundle, was Wat.

"Figured you'd come lookin'," he said. "Been any of the others, I'd just a kept from sight. You, I wanted you to see me. I wanted you to see what you was up against."

"Mr. Luther, you are a very foolish man. If I were you, I'd leave now, while you have the chance. Mr. Boone and Mr. Fenton will be looking for me soon. I am afraid they both have rather short tempers."

"They do, do they?" He chuckled without humor. "I reckon I can handle the both of them, settin' back here like I'm gonna be. Settin' waitin' for them."

"I should think, Mr. Luther, that your first experience with us would have been enough. One would think that anybody of intelligence would stay away."

"I came to get even. I'm a gonna start with you an' this boy. I'm goin' to let you see what I do to him, an' then I'll do worse to you."

"Mr. Luther, will you go now? They are expecting me back at the station. I am afraid I cannot wait any longer."

Oddly, she was not frightened. She knew what she must do and that she had no choice. He was big, a hulking brute, and she hoped—

"You can't wait no longer? Well, what d'you know? Miss Uppity here can't wait!

"Won't do you no good to scream. I already know that hill just cuts off any sound. You an' me, we're alone."

Desperately, Wat struggled. He almost sat up; then he threw himself at Luther's legs.

Scant, with a bored look, kicked him, then kicked him again.

"Mr. Luther? One more time." Her face was very cold. She felt very poised, very still inside. She had expected it to be different than this, but—

He started toward her, and with one easy motion she drew one of the derringers from her pocket and shot him.

It was totally unexpected. She had no weapon in sight, and Scant Luther was sure that even if she had one, she would not have the courage or the good sense to use it.

The derringer was a .44 caliber, and it had two barrels.

He was no more than fifteen feet away, and the slug staggered him. He backed up two paces. "Why you—!"

She walked around him toward Wat. She paused, the derringer in her hand. "Mr. Luther, I would suggest you take your wound and get somewhere right away. You are going to need help."

"Damn you! You—!"

Her heart was pounding heavily, and she could not seem to swallow, but she held the gun steady. Luther took a step toward her.

"Mr. Luther, I have another barrel. If I must shoot you, I will."

He stared at her, his eyes mean and ugly; then, suddenly, his expression changed. His eyes widened; he gasped, and his skin turned an ugly gray.

"You had best go where you can get help, Mr. Luther. You're going to need it."

He backed away, then started through the brush in a stumbling run. Beyond, through the trees, she caught a glimpse of his horse.

Putting the gun in her pocket, she knelt beside Wat and began to pluck at the knots with nervous fingers. They were very tight.

"Ma'am? There's a jackknife in my hip pocket."

She got it out, opened the big blade, and cut him free. When he stood up, she handed the knife back to him. "Gee, ma'am, you sure fixed ol' Scant! I never seen the like!"

"Let's go home, Wat. I—I don't feel well."

They had reached the station when they met Ridge Fenton, rifle in hand, hurrying toward them. Matty was on the steps of the station.

"We heard a shot," Ridge said. Then he added, suddenly concerned at her appearance, "Ma'am? Are you all right?"

"She shot Scant Luther!" Wat exclaimed. "Shot him right through the brisket!"

"You shot Scant?" Fenton was incredulous. "What—?"

"Please! Not now. I want to lie down. Matty—!"

"Sure, mum. You come along with me now." With an arm around her waist, Matty took her inside. "You just sit down now, mum. A cup of hot tea, that's what you need. It's been a shock."

The cup rattled against the saucer when she took it. A swallow, then another.

"Matty, it was awful! Awful! That man—he had poor Wat all tied up. He was planning to kill me. He was going to kill Wat first, and then—"

"Don't talk about it, mum. It's done. It's over an' done with." Matty added tea to her cup. "Mum? There's another thing to think about."

"What's that?"

"You did it, mum. You met him face to face, and when you had to defend yourself, you did it. You stood right on your own two feet and looked him right in the eye, and when there was no help for it, you shot him.

"It is not easy for a woman to be alone, mum, but you did what had to be done. Nothing can take that away from you, and believe me, nobody is goin' to feel sorry that you shot Scant Luther."

She shuddered. "I think—I'm going to lie down, Matty. I hate to leave you with everything to be done, but I'm afraid I—"

"You just go lie down. Peg an' me, we'll handle it. Won't we, Peg?"

"Yes, we will." She ran for the sideboard. "I'll set the table."

With Matty beside her, she crossed to the house and lay down on the bed. Matty returned to the station, and she lay for a long time, staring up at the ceiling.

She had shot a man.

It was unbelievable. She—Mary Claybourne, Mary Breydon, had actually shot a man with a pistol.

It was long after dark when she awakened. She lay still for a minute, listening. Lights were on in the station, and several horses were tied at the corral.

Lighting a match, she lifted the chimney from the lamp and touched the match to the wick. When it caught, she replaced the chimney and looked at herself in the mirror.

She looked a sight, and there were people at the station. Suddenly, she remembered.

She had not reloaded the empty barrel after the gun was fired. Her father had taught her that, and she had heard Temple Boone mention it, also. She got a cartridge and reloaded the gun, glad the derringer was so easily loaded. Her larger gun was cap and ball and took more time. Some of the older men did not like what they called the "newfangled" guns.

She crossed the street to the station.

Mark Stacy was sitting at the table when she entered. With him was Preston Collier. Both men got to their feet promptly.

Temple Boone was there, also, tall, lean, and quiet; his eyes searched her face.

"Mrs. Breydon!" Stacy said. "We've been told what happened! Please join us. We've been worried about you, very worried."

"Why? It is all over now."

"We just wish it were," Collier said, "but we've had word there's trouble coming, serious trouble."

She smiled suddenly. "We've had trouble here, Mr. Collier, and we've handled it. Whatever is coming, we can handle that, too!"

TWENTY-TWO

"**M**rs. Breydon, Temple Boone has assured us you are not
easily frightened, so we are going to place the matter
before you.

"This is Monday. On Saturday next, there will be a stage
leaving Denver carrying at least six men. Four of these men
have already paid their fares and are completing their business
before starting for Laramie.

"We know, and others know as well, that these men will be
carrying rather large sums of money. These men will ride a
special stage accompanying the usual run. They are en route to
California.

"We also have learned that Denver Cross is aware of this and
plans to rob both stages, and if our information is correct, he
plans to do it here.

"It seems," Collier added, "that he intends to take care of
some unfinished business here at the same time."

"How many men will he have? Denver Cross, I mean?"

"We understand there will be six men involved, and we will
be prepared for them."

"I think he will have more than that," Mary Breydon said. "I think he will have twice that many."

Collier smiled, shaking his head. "We know who the men are. We also know that is all he has. We know Mercer will be there, and Williams, of course. Neff is believed to be one of them—"

"He won't be there," Temple Boone said.

They glanced up at him. "He won't be able to make it," Boone said.

"Nevertheless," Collier persisted, "we understand there will be six men." He glanced over at Mary. "I am involved because two of the men traveling west are business associates of mine who are also friends. I want nothing to happen to them."

"I want nothing to happen to anyone at my station," Mary said.

"Of course," Collier agreed. "The point is that we expect to have a reception committee awaiting the outlaws, and we would like you and your family to be in Laporte."

"No."

"What?"

"No," Mary said. "This is my station, and it is my responsibility. I will not be away when there is to be trouble."

"We want no harm to come to you, nor your daughter."

"Neither do I, but my place is here. Also, as you must realize, the outlaws would know we were gone and would immediately suspect something was wrong.

"No, gentlemen, our place is here, and this is where we will be. There may be injuries. The passengers will certainly wish to be fed. Now unless I am mistaken, the outlaws will have one or more men inside the station before the trouble begins."

"That's good thinking, Mrs. Breydon." Mark Stacy turned to Collier. "Of course, she's right. They will have a couple of riders, men strange to Mrs. Breydon, probably, or at least men who will keep her attention on them, waiting here in the station."

Temple Boone straddled a chair. "Look," he suggested. "How are they going to do it? Come charging in here a-horseback, alerting everybody that something is about to happen?

"I think Mrs. Breydon is right. Suppose they have two men

eating in here, innocent as babes. Another man could be getting Ridge Fenton to fix a horseshoe for him or some other little chore.

"They'll know all about Ridge. He always talks peace and is readier for a fight than any man I know. They'll want one or two men there to put him out of action.

"A couple of others might come shagging down the pike and ride over to the corral just before the stage comes in. They'd have Ridge out of action, they'd have Mrs. Breydon and Matty Maginnis locked up, and they could open fire on the stage from three directions."

"Open fire?" Collier exclaimed. "This is to be a holdup. Why should they open fire?"

"Mr. Boone is right," Mary said. "We know who some of these men are. They are former guerrillas, and they kill the weak and helpless as well as others. They will want no witnesses left alive to testify against them or to identify them."

"Mrs. Breydon," Collier said, "I am going to insist that you be away from here. You could go to my ranch. You'd be safe there—"

"No, Mr. Collier. A year ago, I might have done just that, but a lot has happened this past year, both before I came here and since. I will be here, where I should be."

Mark Stacy interrupted. "Mrs. Breydon? You can be here if you wish, although the stage company certainly does not expect it of you, but if you are to be here, promise me that you'll all get into Matty's room with the door locked the minute that stage rolls into the yard.

"You see," he said, "that stage will be loaded with deputies, heavily armed, waiting for trouble. That stage is strongly built, and my men will all have shotguns."

"They'll be watching the stage when the passengers get aboard in Laporte," Boone said.

Collier smiled. "Of course. But the passengers they encounter will be a different group of men. Don't worry, Boone. They'll be surprised. We'll get the lot of them."

Tuesday passed quietly, and Wednesday, yet Mary could feel the tension building within her. Had she been foolish? How could she dare risk the lives of Peg and Wat? Or of Matty?

Or even to allow the children to see such a thing or be close to it. No matter what took place, men would be killed or injured, and with all that shooting going on, there was no telling who might be killed.

"Matty," she said when they were alone, "I am frightened."

"I know, mum. I feel just the same. 'Tis a power of wickedness there is in the world, and too bad that the likes of you an' me must suffer for it. You could go, mum. I'd stay.

"I'm not suggestin' you're afraid, but it's just that my life has been rougher than yours. I'm used to it now. I'd not want you or Peg to see what will happen."

"No, Matty. This is where I belong. If a man was station agent here, wouldn't he be expected to stay?"

On Thursday, the people on the stage were a friendly lot, laughing and gay. They were part of a traveling show that was to perform in Denver.

"You've the best food on the line, miss," the show's manager said. "I wish we could stay over."

"We've been told there will be sleeping quarters here next year," she said.

"Good! I'll vote for it if you're still here to do the cooking." He glanced at Matty. "Or is it you?"

" 'Tis the both of us," Matty said. "If we should come into Denver, could we see the show?"

"I'll seat you myself!" he said gallantly.

Temple Boone stopped by late on Friday. He took a cup and filled it, then said, "We can't persuade you?"

"No," she said.

Wat had been dunking a doughnut. He looked up and started to speak, but Matty interrupted.

"You said that Jordy Neff would not be one of them. How could you know such a thing?"

Boone sipped his coffee. "Jordy ain't the brightest one around, but he's cunning, like an animal. He's not going to get into any situation somebody else sets up. He'll be in Laporte in plain sight. You mark my words. He's like a coyote, wary of traps."

"It ain't gonna work nohow," Wat said. "That Mr. Collier, he doesn't know that bunch."

Mary was suddenly all attention, and so was Boone. There was something in the way he spoke—

"Why do you say that, Wat?" she asked.

"Why, those fellers! They been doin' this for years! D'you suppose they ain't seen Collier talkin' to Stacy? An' to those others? Sure, they know something's gone haywire. They got men in that lot that can smell trouble as far as Jordy Neff.

"Don't you suppose they've got it all figured out? And *six* men? That ain't the way Denver Cross works, nor his boss, either. There'll be twenty men, maybe more."

"Twenty? But Mr. Collier said there would be but six—"

"Where d'you suppose he heard that? Who d'you suppose tipped them off in the first place?"

"Wat? What do you know about this?" Mary asked.

"When you all were talkin' the other night, I listened," he said. "I know I wasn't s'posed to, but I done it.

"When Mr. Collier rode up here with Mark Stacy, I knowed somethin' was in the wind. I just set there wonderin' how growed-up men could be so foolish. They got a tip. I can just bet who supplied that tip! I also could make a good bet where they got the idea he'd only six men. I know there's at least twenty, maybe more."

"How could you know that?" Mary asked.

"You all kep' askin' where I come from. I lived over yonder near Bonnar Springs. Them outlaws was usin' my pa's ranch for a hideout. I *seen* all those men layin' about up there, gamblin', killin' time, waitin' until somebody decides it's a proper time to use them.

"Some of them moved in a good while back. Then a lot come in a bunch just about the time that Flandrau killed your man.

"Those fellers know what they are doin'. They been through all this many a time. I've heard 'em talk. Just about everything's been tried on 'em before this, so they know what to expect.

"They are *bloody*, ma'am. They don't care how many they kill. Look what happened back to Lawrenceville.

"I like ol' Wilbur, an' he'll be a settin' up there in plain sight, one of the first to get shot. They'll kill 'em all, and your Mr. Collier along with it."

"Wat, how can you be sure?"

He glanced around at her. "Ma'am, I heard 'em talk. They paid me no mind. I was just a no-account youngster hangin' around. It wasn't until after I left there that some of them began to worry for fear I heard too much."

"What will they do, Wat?"

"I been studyin' about that, ma'am, but I surely don't know. Only I know they'll do what is least expected. Like killin' Mr. Collier. He doesn't expect that, an' neither do you, but I'll bet they been studyin' how they can do that an' let it be accidental-like. Sort of an innocent bystander."

"Why should they want to kill him?"

"If Flandrau still calculates on running for office," Boone said, "Collier would oppose him, and Collier has a lot of power."

"But what will they do? If Wat is right—"

"We've got to believe he is. Look, the boy hung around up there for at least a year, maybe longer, just listening to them talk, plan, and connive. Or listening to them talk about what they'd done or how they would do it. He knows a lot more about what they think than either one of us."

Yet when she turned down the lamp and blew it out, she was no closer to a solution.

She stood for a moment looking out on the gray area where the stage would stop. What would they do? What could they do?

Lying on her back in bed, with Peg sleeping on the cot nearby, she stared up into the darkness. What would they do? What could they do?

She tried to remember the long talks her father had with various army officers who stopped at the Oaks, when they had talked about surprises, about tactics, about the battles of the Revolution. Couldn't there be a clue in some of that?

What were the dangers they must face? If the stage was to be robbed here and the men killed, what was there the outlaws must fear?

Surprise would be in their favor, yet if Wat was right and they had deliberately allowed Stacy or Collier to be tipped off on the robbery, the surprise was lost. So why the tip-off?

To mislead Stacy and Collier. Mislead them how? If they were warned of the attack—?

She sat up suddenly. *To mislead them as to where the attack was to take place!*

But where, then? If not here, where?

Along the trail? But if Wat was right and they planned on killing Preston Collier, how could they do that? He would not be on the trail, and he would not be on the stage. The chances were that he would be at the ranch.

Of course!

It was almost daylight. Rising quickly, careful not to awaken Peg, she began to dress. As she dressed, her thoughts returned to their immediate problem.

What were the risks the outlaws would take? What must they guard against if their plan was to succeed?

An attack on Collier's ranch would be a complete surprise unless she could warn them in time. But they would be depending on surprise, and the attack would be totally unexpected.

Certainly, they would see the men they wanted board the stage. They had arranged to have Collier and Stacy warned against an attack. Of course, the attack would not be on the trail. That would not account for Collier, and there would be too much chance in that wide open country of being seen.

The stage then would stop at Collier's. The travelers would dismount to be entertained, and some deputies or something of the kind would board the stage and pull out. The attack would come then, the attack and the robbery, not only of the stage passengers but of Collier's ranch home.

And then they would come here. As no attack had developed, the deputies would be off guard.

What risk remained that the outlaws must guard against? The answer was all too simple.

Ridge Fenton and Temple Boone!

TWENTY-THREE

When she walked into the station, she began at once to prepare breakfast. As she worked, she was thinking, realizing what she must do and that so little time remained.

Stepping to the door, she saw Ridge Fenton approaching the station.

"Mr. Fenton? Will you do me a favor? Saddle Nimrod, the horse I recovered from Jordy Neff. Saddle him and bring him to the door."

He merely glanced at her, then turned and walked back to the barn. By the time she had the coffee ready, Fenton was back, and Temple Boone was with him.

"Mr. Boone? I have been thinking about things, and I believe there will be an attempt to kill you and probably Mr. Fenton before the stage comes in."

Boone nodded. "I been thinkin' the same thing. What's the horse for?"

"I'm riding over to Collier's. I had time to think last night, and I believe they will hit there first. I believe, as Wat does, that they tipped Mark Stacy and Preston Collier purposely, guessing what his reaction would be."

"They couldn't count on what he'd do, ma'am."

"Yes, they could. They would decide he would either do what he has done or try to surround the stage with guards. I am sure they have planned for that, too."

"He's got soldiers, ma'am. They came through here after midnight, headed for the Collier place. I talked with 'em. Their sergeant asked to be remembered to you, ma'am. His name was Barry Owen."

"Good! He knows some of these men by sight. And he knows Flandrau."

"He's got seven men with him. Veterans, he said, mostly from the Indian wars. They sized up like a tough bunch."

She took off her apron.

"Please, ma'am? Better let me go."

"You? I need you here. You and Mr. Fenton. Without you, there'd be nobody."

"Wat could ride over there."

"Yes, he could, but I am not sure they would believe him, and they must! They must believe!"

"Wait a minute, ma'am. You can't go now. Here comes Jordy Neff!" Boone studied the hillside, the area around the blacksmith shop, the corrals.

"Ridge, I'm going out to meet him. He wants me himself, but I'm betting there's somebody else hid out around. I'll trust you to take care of him."

"I can't see through brush! What d'you think I am?"

"A damned good man, and a canny one. If there's anybody out there, he's yours."

Jordy Neff was tying his horse to the corral; then he started toward the station. Temple Boone did not wait but stepped out quickly. "Jordy! You lookin' for me?"

Mary Breydon had heard of gunfights, but she had never actually seen one, and she scarcely saw this.

Neff was startled. He had expected to get closer, had expected to surprise Boone, had planned the words he was going to say. It was a story he planned to tell, and he wanted it to sound right. He wanted it to be dramatic. He was going to call Boone and—

He had demanded this job, insisted on it. He wanted to kill Boone and wanted the name of having killed him. He was thinking of that as he started toward the station, thinking of that when he should have been concentrating on Boone.

He started to reply, started reaching for those fancy words when he should have been reaching for his gun.

Automatically, his hand did drop; he gripped the butt, and then something slammed him in the chest. The blow staggered him. His gun came up hip high, arm extended, hammer back and sliding off his thumb.

The second bullet caught him on the inside of his elbow, glancing off into his side. His own bullet, deflected, went into the dust.

Neff did a border switch, catching the gun deftly with his left hand as another gun boomed in the background. His mind worked with complete clarity now. He knew he had been hit twice, and the last one had broken his elbow. As he caught the gun in his left hand, he fired, saw Boone twitch, and eared back the hammer.

Two bullets, so closely fired they sounded with one report, hit Neff in the chest, and he fell, dropping his gun.

He rolled over, trying to rise, groping for a gun that lay just out of reach. His arm gave way under him, and he rolled over on his back, staring up at the sky.

He'd better not lie here. It was getting dark, and it was going to rain. What was he doing? Lying out in the dirt like this? A big drop hit him in the face; then several others fell into his eyes, but they were wide open, staring up at the sky, and they did not blink.

Mary Breydon clutched the windowsill where she stood, staring, her heart pounding. Yet—it was over, all over. How long had it been? A minute? Two minutes?

Temple Boone had done this. He had killed this man, yet the man had come to kill him. She must remember that. And the man who lay dead out there had been one of those who destroyed her home in Virginia. He had stolen her horse, and a man allied to him had killed her husband.

"I must go," she said. "I must go or I will be too late."

She turned to Matty. "Don't let Peg see him. Please don't."

Ridge Fenton was at the door. "Don't worry, we'll have him out of sight in no time. Won't do to have him lyin' there when those others come in with the stage."

He looked at her again. "Are you comin' back, ma'am? I mean, after you tell them?"

"If I can, Mr. Fenton, if I can."

She had forgotten how good a horse Nimrod was, and even after so long a time, he seemed to recognize his name and even her.

As she left the station, Wat came out to her. "Ma'am, there's a trail through the woods. They won't see you if you take it, and it's quicker. Cut the time by maybe fifteen minutes!"

She was gone, making the turn into the brush at the point mentioned. Actually, what Wat called a woods was merely a few scattered trees and some patches of brush along some low ground where there had once been a stream. Yet the old trail was good, and Nimrod fancied it. She started off at a good pace and kept the horse to it. One thing she was thankful for. Jordy Neff had known a good horse and had cared for it.

She left her horse tethered behind the house and came in through the garden. The first person she met was Regina, who was coming down a stairway from the rooms above.

"You! What in the world—!"

"Where is your father? I must see him at once!"

Mutely, Regina pointed toward the library and stepped aside.

Mark Stacy, Preston Collier, and Sgt. Barry Owen were there. Swiftly and as concisely as she could, she explained the situation.

"You mean to tell me you believe they will attack *here?*" Collier inquired skeptically.

"It's like them, sir," Owen said. "Mrs. Breydon knows them, sir, as I do. They're a bad lot."

The stage rolled in, and the passengers dismounted. Quickly, four of the soldiers got in. "The rest of you wait here. We'll go down around the bend, drop into that fold in the hills, and then we'll get out and come back. Maybe we can settle it all right here."

Inside the house, Preston Collier opened his gun cases. He had his own assortment of weapons, hunting rifles, and shotguns. He doled them out, passing cartridges to each one. "Take them alive if we can, but only if we can!"

The stage was scarcely out of sight before three men appeared on the trail, walking their horses. Two more showed at the edge of the park to the east of the house. Then two more riders. The first three continued on along the road until past the house, then turned and trotted their horses forward. The other two turned off abruptly, rode up to the gate, and the two dismounted and came up to the door and knocked.

Now several other riders appeared in view.

Preston Collier opened the door wide, and the two men had guns in their hands. They stared into the muzzles of four double-barreled shotguns. "You'd better drop those guns," Mark Stacy advised.

Nobody but a fool would have taken the chance, and these men were not fools.

"Now just come on in very quietly. Leave the door open for the others. We mustn't appear inhospitable."

The next three came in with a rush to face the same battery of shotguns. Without hesitation, they surrendered.

Denver Cross reined in before the house. It was quiet, too quiet. There were women in there, and if he knew his men, they should be screaming by now. He started toward the house, then drew up. A dozen more of his men were coming along the road.

"Mercer, I think everything's under control. Ride over there and see but don't waste any time. We've got to get along after that stagecoach."

Mercer glanced at Cross, then shrugged. Why didn't he go himself? He'd always wanted to be in at the start. He rode his horse to the steps and called out. All was quiet, so quiet he was suddenly scared. He started to turn his horse when he saw Owen beside the door, just out of sight of anybody but him.

"Get down and come in, man. Come quietly!"

"Like hell!" Mercer swung his horse and went for his gun at the same moment and caught two well-aimed rifle bullets before his draw was completed. He fell; his foot hung briefly in the stirrup, then fell free. His horse trotted off.

Denver Cross swore and slapped the spurs to his horse, yelling to his men.

A volley from the house emptied three saddles, and then Cross was away and running. Rounding a bend, he all but charged into the stage, and Wilbur Pattishal, kneeling atop the stage, gave him a charge of buckshot.

"Neat!" Collier said. "Very neat, indeed, thanks to Mrs. Breydon."

An hour had passed; the soldiers under Sergeant Owen had taken the prisoners away. Mercer and two other men had been buried on the far side of the hill. Cross was still alive, although in a bad way.

"We won't be able to connect Flandrau with any of it, I'm afraid," Stacy said, "unless one of the prisoners will talk."

"I'm not so sure," Collier said. "With the testimony of both Mrs. Breydon and Sergeant Owen as to the previous connection of Flandrau with the outlaws, we may be able to tie him to what happened here." He took out a cigar. "Mrs. Breydon? Do you mind?" He struck a match. "That man who was riding your horse, Mrs. Breydon? If we could get him to talk? Most men will talk to avoid hanging."

"I am afraid he has already avoided it, Mr. Collier. Part of this action was to remove Temple Boone from the scene at Cherokee Station. Jordy Neff attempted it and failed."

"Boone killed him?" Stacy commented. "I am not surprised. Boone is a dangerous man."

"And a gentleman," Mary said.

She got to her feet. "I must ride back to the station. They will be worried."

Collier arose. "It is good to have you for a neighbor, Mrs. Breydon. Please do not become a stranger."

"Thank you."

Mark Stacy got up. "The stage is gone, but if I could borrow a horse, Collier, I'd ride along with Mrs. Breydon. We've some business to discuss."

He took up the rifle with which he had been armed. "We're making a stopover of Cherokee Station. It isn't officially a home station, but the atmosphere is so congenial that our passengers are beginning to insist on it."

Sitting her saddle, she waited for Mark Stacy to join her. The brief spatter of rain had ended, and the clouds were breaking up.

Stacy rode around the corner of the house, and together they started back along the main trail. The air was clear and fresh, and it was a pleasure to be riding. It was almost like old times.

"You've done a fine job, Mrs. Breydon," Stacy said. "Frankly, I had my doubts. I'd heard of women operating stations in California but never really believed it possible. And you—you're scarcely the type."

"What is the type, Mr. Stacy?"

He shrugged. "You've got me there. Only—well, you're a lady."

"I hope so." She smiled again. "I have never found it a handicap."

"This"—he gestured toward the station that was just coming within sight, although still some distance off—"will soon be a thing of the past. They'll be building a railroad west as soon as the war is over. Stage lines will only be feeder lines for a while."

"How long, do you think? I mean before they complete a railroad this far?"

"Three years, perhaps four. Ben Holladay is already thinking of it, and so am I. I've become involved, in fact. That is where the future is, Mrs. Breydon."

They rode on in silence. "And you, Mrs. Breydon? What are your plans?"

"For the moment, to operate Cherokee Station as best I can. When the war is over, we may go back to Virginia. I have property there."

"Some of us would like to keep you here," Stacy said. "This is a new country. We need people of vision, both men and women. And—well, we need *you*."

"Thank you. I am not going to think of that now. I've Peg to think of, and Wat. He's become a member of the family. For a while, I am going to live day by day." From the crest of a low hill, she could see the sunlight on Peg's hair as she stood outside the station. "Later, after I've become adjusted, I may think of other things."

"When do you, I hope you will think of me."

"Of course, Mr. Stacy. How could I help it?"

"Well," he said irritably, "there's Temple Boone."

"Yes, there is, isn't there? As Matty says, he's a fine figure of a man!"

Matty was on the step drying her hands on her apron. Temple Boone and Ridge Fenton were walking in from the barn, and Wat was shading his eyes toward them.

They were all there, at Cherokee Station, and it was good to be coming home.

Several hours later and fifty miles away, Jason Flandrau was heading southeast, avoiding the trails. The money belt around his waist was heavy, as were his saddlebags. He had played out his hand in Colorado, but New Mexico lay to the south, and there was new country to the west of it. It was a wise man who knew when to fold his cards and toss in his hand. Down there or in California, he could deal them his own way, in his own time.

He had been in his office, about to close the window, when he heard them talking in the street. Denver Cross was dead, most of his gang wiped out, but they had some prisoners who, in fear of a hangman's noose, were telling all they knew.

Thirty minutes later, he was in the saddle and finding his way out of town through the back streets.

Now, miles away and safe, he smiled smugly. So much the better! There had been no need to divide the money he had promised, and he could afford to take his time and look around. What he had almost done in Colorado, he could do elsewhere. He rode around the base of a low hill and down to the small creek among the trees. He would water his horse and take a breather.

The Comanche war party was in an irritable mood. They had ridden more than a hundred miles without taking a scalp.

They were stopped by the stream when they heard the sound of a horse's hoofs. The rider was approaching at an easy gait.

They were standing in a half circle with arrows in position and bows bent when the rider came through the trees. He drew up sharply.

There were twelve of them, the first Comanche war party he had ever seen and the last he would ever see. He went for his gun, but the bulging money belt impeded his draw. The Comanches had no such problem.

He was still partly alive when a warrior stooped over him with a scalping knife.

Somebody, he thought, had dealt him a black deuce.